This issue contains stories about cold winter nights, stories about the panic that comes in the dark, stories about awkward house guests, stories about love, stories about diner food, stories about other kinds of food, stories about fairy tales gone rogue, stories about the lies we tell ourselves, stories about the legacies of the dead, and stories about the memories of childhood.

These are the stories which usher us into a new season.

Underland Arcana is published quarterly. This issue is published in conjunction with the first new moon following the spring equinox.

EDITOR
Mark Teppo

COVER IMAGE
Tod Ryan

SIGIL ART
Andrew Penn Romine

PUBLISHER
Underland Press
Clackamas, OR, USA

Hug the darkness before it flees . . .

https://www.underlandarcana.com

UNDERLAND ARCANA

~ 2 ~

Underland Press

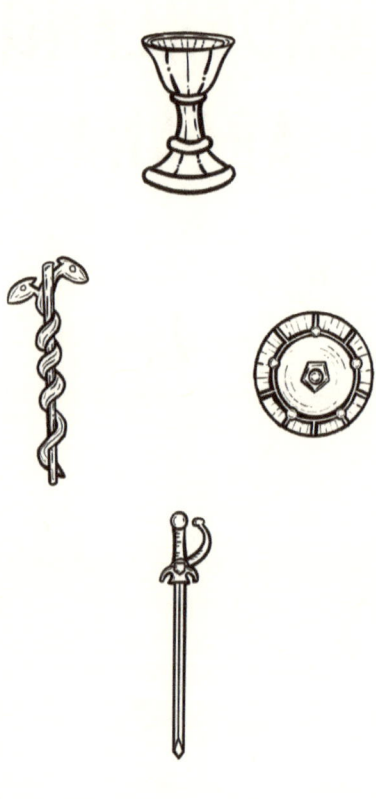

Contents

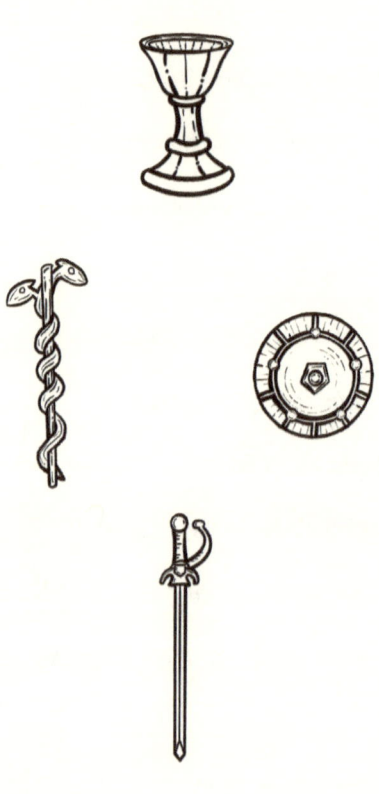

Looking Back

The tarot reveals as much about you as it does about the future, which is to say: when you scry the unknown, something out there sees you too. When we receive a reading from the cards, you'll notice the story that emerges is a story you already know. It's like looking in the mirror and really seeing yourself. You know, the self that has gotten older when you weren't paying attention. The self that looks tired or sad or some other emotion that you don't really want to think about, but man, it's there on your face, isn't it?

Or perhaps when you look, you think: "Damn, that person looks happy." I hope you think that. I do.

Anway, when I put out the call for stories, I didn't want writers to preselect the cards for me. "Let the card find your story." I wanted writers to wander into the weeds with the tarot and come back with interesting things. I didn't want to be swamped with Six of Cups stories, for example.

When I read for *XIII*, the Major Arcana anthology centered around Death, I knew that the horror market listing went up first because the initial wave was all skinwalker stories. That trope is low hanging fruit, frankly, for the card, and it was nice to get all of those out of the way early. What I wanted was what came later, and that was stories about transformation and renewal and rebirth in ways I hadn't even thought about. Because, yes, building these issues is a journey for me as well.

Underland Arcana is a horror market, sure. But it's also a Dark Fantasy market. And a market for Whimsy. And a market for "What the fuck did I just read and why it is still burrowing into my brain?"

I have decided to put images of the cards before the stories, for purely practical reasons. You shouldn't think about them too much, but do remember that the card found the story. Not the other way around.

Mark Teppo
April 12th, 2021

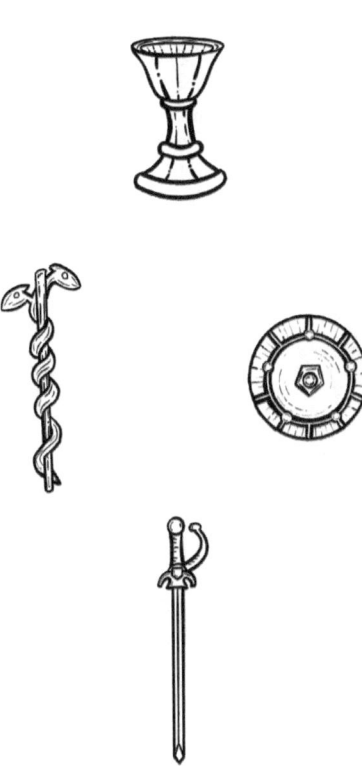

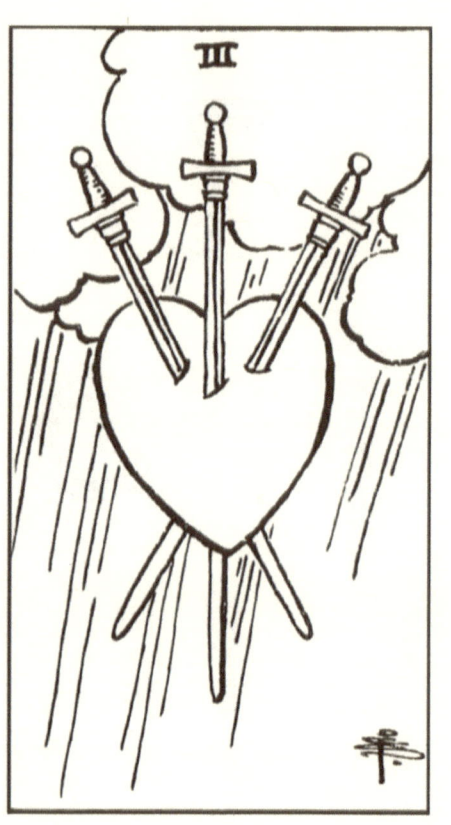

Dog Sitting

~ Jon McGoran

The dog lying at her feet let out a sad, heavy sigh and then the house returned to a silence marred only by the clock on the mantle. The dog's name was Bruce, after the shark in *Jaws*, but Frank only ever called it "The dog." It was the only thing Frank had left her, apart from the debts she'd discovered the day after he died, and a few bruises from the night before.

Frank used to brag about the dog, what a killer it was. "He could tear a grown man to shreds as easy as looking at him," he liked to say. She had always wondered why he needed such a big damn dog, other than that he liked to brag. Now she knew the real reason: The gambling. The drugs. The stealing. People had been after Frank.

But not anymore. A heart attack got to him before any of them could, and there was nothing the dog could do about that.

Frank had loved the dog, as improbable as that seemed. Or as close to love as he was capable. He loved it more than he loved her, that was for sure.

She should have left them both, back when she still had a chance. She could have made a life for herself. Not much of one, probably, but something. Something better than this.

The dog rolled onto its side, the big spiked collar scraping against the floor.

The room was getting dark again now, shadows seeping into the corners, pooling on the floor, like a leaky boat sinking into dark water. She could reach the lamp on the table, but she didn't dare. There was still enough light that she could see the dog's eyes looking up at her, watching, unreadable, never leaving her. They seemed to her more like the eyes of a reptile than man's best friend. But man's best friend it had been—Frank's partner in crime, literally.

The pins and needles in her feet had gone away hours earlier, and she'd made peace with the itchy spot on her arm that she didn't dare scratch. But the cramp in her leg was back, even worse than before. She flexed her foot just an inch to relieve it, rustling the damp fabric of the dress she'd been wearing since what had passed as a funeral the day before.

The dog showed its teeth again, giving her that hungry look and that low, throaty growl, the one that used to earn a clout from Frank and a stern, "Knock it off."

The dog had actually listened to Frank, too. But only him.

Now Frank was gone, and the dog was still here.

It was almost dark when the clock began to chime. It was eight o'clock. Well past feeding time.

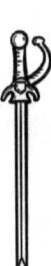

KNIGHT of CUPS.

Reggie

~ *Nathan Batchelor*

The sound coming from the guitar amp was interference, I told Maggie, opening the door of the closet where we kept Reggie's things. The smell of him was still here. Pencil lead and the lightest touch of mole. You could never get that scent out of a man born in mole country.

"It could be spies," Maggie said.

"It's not spies," I said.

"Russian spies," Maggie said. "or Chinese."

"This is Canada, hon," I said. "We'll check the radio stations. What we're hearing is sure to be from there."

"Still, Boston is close. There has to be important things there, right?"

I kept hearing the click of her tongue ring, while I dug through Reggie's things. Here was a medal from a 5k race, third place, just a year ago. Here was his undergrad thesis, titled *The Composition of Dung Balls in the Canadian Dung Beetle*. Here was a photo of him as a child, pushing a mole on a swing set, the mole's face set in fear. When I asked him about it, he said the mole was so scared that he snapped the chain with his grip after the photo was taken.

"Do you want me to help?" Maggie asked.

I forgot sometimes I had no hands. Birth defect. One arm ended at the elbow. For the other, there was a wrist that terminated in a ball of flesh without fingers. I had learned to manage, and with some setup could do just about anything someone born with two hands could.

"Go ahead," I said.

It gave me time to think. I hated puzzles, at the same time, it was the most excited I'd seen my daughter since she'd stopped helping me make cookies, before she wore black lipstick, before I found the scars on her arms.

Moving the amp around did get rid of the interference. That was enough for me, but Maggie, like her father, *had* to know what the interference was.

After she'd dragged out the boombox, we sat around it in the living room and clicked from station to station.

"It's none of them," Maggie said.

This wasn't something I could let go of. My daughter was growing away, doing things her father never would have approved of. I needed this. She needed this.

"I'll ask at work," I said.

"But you teach anatomy."

"I still have friends in other departments, Maggie."

I hardly knew anyone in the physics department, except for Dr. Blagg, who I knew because we were on the committee for students with disabilities. He stared at equations of gravity all day, but he would know enough to help us.

On Monday, I found him in his office, aroma of chalk and coffee. His pants were spotted with white handprints.

"It's not spies," he said, after I explained the situation to him.

"Of course, it isn't. But will you come look?" I asked. "Please," I must have sounded a little desperate. "For my daughter."

He came Friday evening. He squatted by the amp with his ear next to it. Maggie sat on the edge of the couch with a notebook, writing, though I knew not what. They looked ridiculous. There was some part of my heart that tugged for Blagg. I had made him dinner and was prepared to entertain the notion of some kind of unspoken gift, perhaps a brush on the arm, a date, even a kiss. He wasn't a bad looking man. But he hadn't expected any of that. Nor did he seem all business. He seemed to take an interest to Maggie. Asking her questions about her life that seemed to excite her. Something I had not done in a long time.

"What are you doing?" I asked her.

"Trying to write down what they say," she said.

"They?"

"It's more than one person. Can't you tell?"

I couldn't. I wasn't even sure that the sounds were even human.

"I'll be back," Blagg said. "I can't hear anything either."

He came back with an electrical device from his car. "We'll just hook this up to the amp. It'll record the sounds. I'll clean up the audio this weekend."

After he left, I washed the dishes, the sound of laughter extinguished, nothing but the hum of the air conditioner. The silence bothered me so much that before I went to bed, I turned the amp on for a little while. But I could make out nothing.

When Dr. Blagg didn't call on Monday, I wasn't worried. He was a busy academic. But he wasn't there for the committee meeting on Thursday either. Later, when I called him, it went to voicemail. But when I called the secretary of the department, she had said he had missed no classes. I prayed nothing was wrong.

When I asked Maggie if she had figured out what was being said, she said nothing, but in a curious way that would set off any mother's alarm. After she'd gone to bed that night, I browsed her notebook. She had written a script out of the noise. Speaker one and speaker two. Syllables and words randomly placed. There was a single word circled. Dad.

I didn't feel anger, so much as sympathy. There were stories of children acting out fantasies about their dead parents, but I had thought my own Maggie would be immune. The therapist said her turn to darker things was nothing but a phase, that I should support her in whatever she wanted to do, even if it wasn't something Reggie would have agreed with.

"People change," the therapist had said. "Perhaps he would ask her what she wants."

I doubted that's what Reggie would have wanted. I put the notebook back where I left it. I would call the doctor in the morning.

☉

"I really don't want to say," Dr. Blagg said when I'd finally tracked him down on campus. "It's not certain at all really."

His feet were slanted away from me, and when the lightest rain began to fall in front of the physics building, he started to walk away. I followed him. I had not brought an umbrella. They were awkward to use without hands.

"I don't understand," I said. "Are you saying the message is some kind of secret thing?"

"There's two options," he said. "Either you're in on the joke, or you're not."

"What joke?" I said. "I'm asking you honestly here, as a mother concerned for her daughter. Why can't you just tell me?"

The wind picked up and blew his combover erect.

"You know I've never been able to smell the rain," He said. "Everyone knows when it's coming. Except me. I've never been able to."

He wrote an address down on a notepad and handed it to me.

"This is where the signal originates. Perhaps it's some relatives of his playing a joke with your daughter."

"Relatives of who? Reggie?"

He nodded. "You'll have to ask your daughter how she did it. Beats me why she'd go to such trouble."

It wasn't until I was back in the car that I looked up the address. It was in mole country.

☉

I waited for Maggie to get out of school that day. I hadn't picked her up in years. There was a new section on the school, one I didn't recognize. When Maggie came out, it took me a minute to pick her out among the other kids. She walked like her father's sisters, a bounce in her step that reminded me of Judy and Nancy, who both lived in Chicago. Not at all like the girl she had been, years before.

"Where are we going?" she said.

"Mole country," I said. "For the weekend. Where your father grew up."

She smiled.

The problem with mole country was that the maps barely help. Roads end and begin without reason. Roads may be horse trails, service roads, or abandoned mole tunnel toppers. And when you forget to download the maps, like I did, only the gray and green spaces greet you. When my phone lost service a hundred kilometers away from any major highway, I pulled over on the side of the road.

Maggie sat on the top of the car with her jacket off. It was warmer here, and the trees were not yet completely naked of their leaves. We had seen a mole walking up the road, a bucket on his arm full of apples, resting on his cane as he paused to peer at our car. Maggie had watched him with the requisite amazement.

She held the maps while I tried to match up the roads between what was on my phone and the map we'd picked up at the first gas station in the province.

"Not to be mean, Mom. But shouldn't you be better at this. You're a professor and all."

"There are a lot of things I should be better at," I said. "But you'll just have to deal with me."

I was losing my patience. This place wasn't dangerous. The rumors of people being lost and eyes being harvested by the moles were exaggerated. There had only been one case of that, nearly a hundred years ago. Reggie had told me in detail, as his adopted mole parents had told him. It was better for her not to hear of such stories. That would only make things worse between us.

"Do you think a mole will try to take our eyes?" she said.

We sat in the car a long time before I decided to go into the convenience store. I left Maggie there. She was still fuming from an argument we'd had about where to go. I let her know that I was just inside, that there was pepper spray in the glove compartment. We hadn't taken the self-defense course that long ago, and the instructor said Maggie was a natural at combat, which had bothered me at the time, but now I felt thankful.

"Hello?" I said.

There was a mole wedged between two shelves, the top half of his torso inside the hole in the ground, just like, well, a mole. It was every run-down shop in every run-down mole town. The musky scent. The cellar door, where moles who preferred to travel underground could

enter and exit. Two aisles worth of monocles, glasses, and lorgnettes for the nearsighted creatures. Spiced
strips of flypaper swaying in the breeze from the buzzing
air conditioner. The sound or tremor of my steps must
have alerted the mole. His butt wiggled.

"What? You finally find that flathead screwdriver?" the
mole with his head in the floor said.

"No," another voice said, this one much older, feebler.
"We got a guest, Paul."

I hadn't seen the mole behind the counter, straining his
eyes out of disbelief at this woman without arms standing in his store in the middle of nowhere. His fur was
coal black. The lenses of his glasses were as thick as they
were round.

"Be right with you," Paul said.

"That's okay," I said. "I don't mean to interrupt. I really
don't need anything at all. Just some questions."

The mole behind the counter clicked his tongue. Was
that a mole message? Perhaps a sound of warning. I
wished I had come here more with Reggie. Though he
had never wanted me to see the place he grew up.

"You some kind of cop?" Paul asked.

"She doesn't have any arms," the older mole said.

"Well, that don't mean she can't be a cop, Mason," Paul said.
"Mr. Sudduth had his legs cut off in the war and he is a cop."

"Was a cop," the older mole said. "Died last winter.
Cancer."

"No, I'm not a cop. I work at the university. In Toronto.
But I knew Reggie," I said, hoping their eyes would light

up in recognition, thinking the stories were true that everyone in this part of the country knew each other by name.

I repeated Reggie's name, the full one, mentioning his adopted parents, his sisters. "He was my husband."

Mason's head swiveled. I glanced back at the car. Maggie's feet were up on the dashboard.

"He's the one hit by the car, right, Paul?"

"It was a truck. Reggie was Leonard's cousin," Paul said.

I didn't know a Leonard. I found myself holding my breath. Then caught myself. How foolish to think these moles would know something of Reggie's death, something that would tie things up in a pretty bow.

"Weren't you there, Paul?" Mason said.

Paul stopped wiping his hands on a rag black with earth. I couldn't tell if his hands were getting cleaner or dirtier.

He looked at me, then back at the old mole. "Say miss, would you care for some fly juice?"

There were chairs out back, hand-carved from mud like they sold in the department stores in the city, except these were the real thing, chairs shaped by powerful mole hands. I worried that my pants would get dirty, but Paul reassured me. Awkwardly, he handed me a soda. I had passed on the fly juice. He pointed to the chair. A delicateness in his hands reminded me of Reggie.

"It won't dirty you up," he said. "The chair, I mean. You coming, Mason?"

"To hell with your breaks. Someone's got to work," Mason called through the open door.

Paul sipped his spiced fly juice.

"I saw the truck pull out, strike your husband's car on the side," he said. "I was working on the subterranean road at the time. Volunteer Tunnelers' Association."

"I've heard of it," I said.

"It was about noon. I was on break," he said. "My eyesight's a lot better than that old mole in there. Vitamins."

"It was a mole driving," I said.

He licked his lips and rubbed his eyes. "It was."

"I'm sorry, I didn't mean it like that," I said. "The driver's name was Arthur. Did you know him?"

"There's lots of people I don't know around here ma'am. Maybe it's better if you just say what you came to say."

What had I come to say?

"I'm sorry," I said. I had offended him. "My daughter has found something."

He leaned forward. I explained the radio signals, the amp. I thought I droned on, but he never looked away. He never looked at my arms either. He never seemed to notice my disability.

"You say the signal is from here?" he said.

"Yes," I said.

"That would make some kind of sense." He rubbed his chin. "We are spies after all."

I thought I had misheard. I felt an unease in my chest.

"I'm joking," he said.

And then laughter came bursting out of me.

He said, "Would you like to see him?"

"Arthur? The man who hit him?" I said.

"No. Your husband," he said. "Well, what's left of him anyway."

Reggie's sisters had identified his body before my plane returned from an academic conference. I only saw him after the morticians were done with him and only from the neck down.

"It's better this way," his sister Judy had said.

It was dark in the tunnel with Paul. The musty smell was overwhelming. Chicken feed, dried corn, tubs of sawdust and stacks of firewood glowed green in the sight of the night-vision goggles he had given me.

"I kept it in here. Things last longer inside the Earth," he said setting aside what must have been some kind of mole scarecrow.

After he turned on a light, and I removed my goggles, he offered me a ball of something. Teeth, hair, pencil shavings protruded from a something that resembled mud.

"What is it?" I said.

"I found this at the site of your husband's wreck. I was wearing headphones, and they were picking up some noise. Voices I thought. But when I came back here, the sounds had stopped."

Paul flipped on what looked like a baby monitor. I could hear voices under the static.

"Maybe this is your signal. I never put it and your husband together until you came in. I just thought it was some trinket thrown out a window," he said. "Perhaps his presence amplified the signal somehow. Perhaps your presence works the same way. Yes, that must be it."

I thanked him, though I knew he was caught up in a kind of mole superstition that Reggie and I would never believe in.

"If you want, I can let you talk to the Matron. She'd know more," he said.

"But what is it? Why do you say this thing is him?"

"It's a dung ball," he said, "made by beetles. But I figure he made one. Probably not with dung or it would stink to high heaven. But it's probably his teeth and stuff there."

"That doesn't make any sense. He studied beetles but he wasn't crazy."

"Maybe he wasn't crazy. Maybe it was something he believed in. I don't know what else to tell you," Paul said.

Maggie was in a better mood when I returned to the car. We stopped at a diner run by moles. The food was so greasy I could barely eat it. She picked over mac and cheese.

"The trip isn't completely wasted," she said. "Do you know where Dad lived?"

"He would never tell me exactly," I said. "He was ashamed." I was suddenly not at all hungry. "Let's go home."

"But I'm still eating."

"We're leaving," I said.

I almost threw the ball away then. Reggie wouldn't carry such a strange thing. He wasn't the kind to carry things. He even hated carrying wallets. And I knew enough of physics to know balls of dung didn't give off radio waves.

I would put it away with his things when I returned home. The ball would serve as a reminder of the danger of wishful thinking.

If the signal was still there, I was going to get rid of it somehow.

That night, after Maggie had gone to bed, I switched on the amp. I marveled at the setup Maggie had made around it, almost an altar, with pen, paper, headphones, cups of coffee with just slivers of black in the bottom. I heard no voices, no interference.

I drank wine to celebrate. I put the ball away in the closet with the rest of Reggie's things and went to sleep. Some part of me would miss the adventure, the bond with Maggie. But this had all been myth and circumstance.

Then the next morning, when I came downstairs, Maggie was sitting on the couch, the amp was on, and voices were coming out of it. Clear voices. Mine and hers. We were arguing.

"What will we do with Dad's body? Bury him?" Maggie said.

"Yes," I said.

"Again? This has to mean something."

"There is nothing else. There is no meaning." I said.

I was screaming. I barely recognized myself. We had never had that argument. I shut off the amp.

"Mom?" Maggie said.

She was holding the ball of dung in her hand. I slapped it away. She drew back, eyes in a way I'd never seen them before. Not showing horror, but anger, enough to coax tears from her eyes. She stomped away. I had underestimated her. She had seen the dung ball, had snuck into my room to get it.

I turned on the amp and sat in the floor. But when I moved the ball, the noise cut away. I couldn't take this. I called 911. But when they asked what they could help me with, I didn't say anything. There was no one who could help.

But perhaps there was. By the time Paul said, "Yes, That's what we'll do," the police officer was knocking on my door.

Paul had given me night-vision goggles again, though these fit worse than the last pair. The Matron's blankets ensconced her and gave her the impression of a child. She was small, withered, and the hairs on her head were like vines spiraling out of control. Paul said she must be more than 200 years old, but I'd had trouble believing it. Until I saw her. The frailness, the scars on her arthritic hands where men had cut off her claws years ago, in bits of history Canadian humans would like to forget.

"Raise me up," she said. Her accent was thick with the old mole language. It took me a moment to understand.

Two girl moles, teenagers I thought, perhaps only a little older than Maggie, pulled on pulleys weaved of roots.

Then the old mole was staring at me, or perhaps she was totally blind and feigning a stare.

"What's the problem?" she said, turning to Paul.

"She's found a dung ball," Paul said.

"My husband, he died and now there's a dung ball that—I can't believe I'm saying this—is broadcasting some kind of message," I said.

Her eyes turned on me with the judgment only old lady moles are capable of.

"A singing ball of shit," she said. "And I thought I'd heard everything."

"I'm sorry," I said. "I came because I don't know what else to do."

"What do you think is going on?" she said.

"I think he left a message for us," I said. "Somehow the dung ball is… him or part of him."

"Then what do you need me for?" she said. Her old face cracked, and a smile formed among the wrinkles. Her arm touched mine. Her grip was so powerful. "It's okay. You're scared."

"But why is this happening?" I said. "Is it because he was raised by moles?"

"I don't know," she said. "We merely collect things. Maybe it's not the fact that he was raised by moles, maybe he is special."

Out of all the things to leave a message of. An argument about a body we'd never seen. Out of all the ways to leave a message. A ball of dung. Perhaps the sounds coming out of the amp were his last thoughts. Yes, that had to be it. But he thought about us arguing? Why?

It was long after midnight that I returned home. I sat the ball down atop the amp and went to the kitchen. When I came back I saw, slumped against the overturned amp, Reggie's body, wearing the same clothes he'd worn the day he died.

It was as if some joke had fallen flat. I felt empty. Reggie's body looked so livid. He looked as if he were only asleep. The ball of dung was gone. Of course, I didn't understand, but I realized, like his death, I was past the point of understanding.

I wrapped the body in sheets as best I could, and picked up the phone, but how could I dial any number? Who could I call? Instead, I crept upstairs. Had Maggie seen him? She slept soundlessly. Of course not, she would have called someone, if not me, then the police.

I didn't know what I should do. If I should call the cops myself and have the body taken away, or if that was precisely not what Reggie wanted. Instead I lay there on the couch, glancing from the amp to the body wrapped in sheets, until I fell asleep.

It felt like I hadn't slept at all when I woke. Maggie was sitting in the floor in front of the amp.

"It's gone," Maggie said. "I've tried moving the amp everywhere and the signal is gone."

Then she sniffled and said, "What will we do with Dad's body? Do we bury him?"

"Yes," I said, reflexively, not even catching what I was doing.

"Again? But this has to mean something."

I was already standing. My jaw wired so tight, I thought if I opened my mouth a scream would emerge that could shatter the world.

But I looked over to the body. I thought of the words of the matron. And then I think I saw my daughter for the first time since Reggie died. There was some magic here. This did mean something. What, I wasn't sure. It was just out of reach. Instead of screaming, I opened my mouth, and words of understanding came out.

"What do you think we should do, Maggie?"

When she looked at me, I knew something had changed between her and I and what was left of her father. I knew what the message meant and why he had left it. He wanted Maggie and I to get on with our lives, no matter how incomplete we felt without him.

"I don't know. But maybe we can talk about it."

Yes, I thought. *That's exactly what we'll do.*

Crossing

~ Jennifer Quail

It is winter. It is always winter.

Marie-Eve has never seen a train on the tracks. As long as she can remember it has been a dead spur, leading somewhere forgotten in the distant hills. Sometimes when Maman is not watching her she stands on the tracks and stares north into the hulking, ancient Laurentian Mountains. Papa says the trains came once, but Maman says they have not come in years. She wonders if she could walk to the mountains, or if they would always remain on the horizon. She never tries.

She never sees a train, either, until the first night she sees the woman.

She does not know what woke her, at first. Someone, Maman or Papa, moving in the kitchen? Or the wind rattling the door of the barn?

She slips from under the covers and pads to the window, the floorboards rough and cold beneath her bare feet. Outside there is a light on a pole above the railroad crossing, casting a sickly green-gold pool to warn the drivers who rarely pass of the trains that never come. Marie-Eve peers out, waiting, not knowing for what. Only knowing it is coming.

The woman walks into the light from the shadows somewhere near the house. She wears a dark, heavy, men's coat and her boots leave deep treaded tracks in the snow. She stops at the edge of the road, where the tracks are level with the pavement. She waits.

A pale circle of light appears in the southern darkness. The train arcs up as if springing out of the ground at the horizon. It races across the frost-bitten rails, black and sleek with the glowing cyclops eye of the engine lamp slicing into the night ahead.

The woman stands, hands crammed deep in the pockets of her coat, watching as the train rushes out of the gloom. Marie-Eve can feel the whole house tremble and she's sure Maman and Papa will wake, or in the barn across the tracks the cattle will start lowing. If it were day they would scatter across the fields, she's sure, tripping over the jagged corn stalks that stubble up through the snow. They've never seen a train here, either.

The long, dark engine rolls past the house but while the floor shakes and she can see the steam hissing from the wheels, Marie-Eve can't hear the engine's rumble or the creak of the brakes. There is no light from the cab, though she thinks she sees a dark shape moving from one side to the other, a form that might be at the window looking back. The whole train is dark, not just with lights dimmed or shades drawn, but painted deeper black than India ink and all the glass darkened, too.

Marie-Eve presses her nose to the window, straining to see the woman between the cars. She should be able to see shadows at least in the pool of the lamp. But a light, the head lamps of a truck coming around the curve, slices across her vision and she has to blink.

When she can see again, the train and the woman are gone. The truck thuds across the grade crossing and disappears, gone up the road, and there are only the tracks gray with frost and the empty pool of lamplight.

Marie-Eve tells her Maman about the train, but not the woman. Maman says Marie-Eve was dreaming, that she'd heard a truck passing on the road, carrying milk cans from the dairy twenty kilometers east to the town twenty kilometers west and in her sleep imagined the rattling was a train. Maman says in the winter it's easy to imagine things, even in your sleep. It is convincing, for now. Comforting.

So much so Marie-Eve does not tell her, or Papa, when five winters later she awakes one night and sees the woman waiting for the train again.

This night, she is in the kitchen, the oil lamp bathing the ice box and the wood stove in a flickering greasy gold. The shadows make Papa's old hunting coat look as if someone is hanging inside it on its hook. Maman left her glasses on the drain board and the reflected glow makes them look like solid disks of shiny metal. Marie-Eve does not dare turn on the electric light. They will not notice a sliver of the pate-de-lac-St-Jean is missing when it's cut for tomorrow's supper, and she will sleep better without quite as much an ache in her stomach, she thinks. But better not to wake them anyway.

Marie-Eve moves on tip-toe, listening to the house breathe around her. Papa says the faint creaks and moans are the dry boards, the wind, but in the dark like this Marie-Eve likes to think she can hear the frost prickling across the walls outside and crackling the window glass.

She thinks she hears the soft padding of feet above her, Maman perhaps going to Marie-Eve's room. The noise is like someone moving to her window, at least, and she blows out the lamp. Now there is only the green-yellow outside from the light at the crossing and she is alone in the dark, frozen as surely as the ground outside. She leans over the sink, pushing back the flour-sack curtain, and looks.

She jumps when the shadow moves from the porch, out of the dark corner into her line of sight as if coming from the door. The woman wears the heavy man's coat, her hands driven deep into the pockets. Her boots leave deep, treaded tracks in the snow. Marie-Eve can see puffs of white where the woman breathes in the knife-sharp cold. But while she can hear the sighing crackles of the frost on the walls and the rush of blood in her ears, she does not hear the footsteps crunch in the snow.

She feels the train approach but does not hear it. From the kitchen, she cannot look down on the tracks, so she cannot see the length of the train, but as the long, black engine glides to a stop she sees the movement in the cab, a figure behind the darkened glass. The figure moves closer, but she cannot see a face, only shadows swathed in deeper shadow.

The shadow, she is certain, looks out at the house.

Now she feels the thrum of the engine deep in her chest, and her mind wills there to be sound, but there is only the usual winter night murmurs. She can't see the woman at the crossing, but as the long locomotive begins to move, she looks for the footprints in the snow. When she looks up again, the train and the woman are gone.

She goes back to bed, still hungry, but at least no one has noticed she is awake. The next morning, before breakfast, she stands on the tracks, staring north, but there are only the distant shadows of the mountains, ancient and empty and too far to reach. There are no footprints in the snow but her own.

The third time, Marie-Eve is fifteen, and she is not in the house. Maman is in the hospital in Chicoutimi, an hour away, and Papa is tired. The chores are late, because they are late getting home to the cold house, but the chores must be done. Someone has to go to the barn with the bucket of hot water to thaw the pump and make sure the cows that have not yet been sold can drink.

Marie-Eve lugs the steaming pail to the wellhead, her breath rasping as loud as Maman's did before she went away. The cold burns into her lungs. Her coat is too small but it can last another winter if it must. It is thin, too, so she thinks that the prickling of the skin of her neck is only the wind brushing its chill hand over her. She will be back inside soon, she thinks, and looks back to the house. There is an oily gold glow from the lamp in the kitchen, but the stirring of an upstairs curtain tells her Papa has gone up, leaving the light for her.

A rush of wind makes the door of the barn rattle on its hinges. She checks, but it remains firmly latched.

When she looks back the woman is walking from the shadow of the porch, her hands buried deep in the pockets of the heavy coat.

Marie-Eve turns without thinking to the south. A pinprick of light is growing, from the size of a star to the beam of a penlight to the glow of a torch to the lamp of the locomotive cutting through the darkness so sharply she thinks it could be a solid blade. From outside, without the safe thickness of glass between her and train, there is a depth to the black cars that has its own gravity. She wants to fall towards them, as if they are a train-shaped void and she is standing on the edge, looking down into some unfathomable abyss.

Something in the abyss moves and she realizes the woman is gone.

Marie-Eve drops the bucket and starts to run, and the train starts to move. The streamlined edges of the cars blur into the darkness, and she cannot say where the cars ends and their shadows on the snow begins. The silence pulls the sounds of the night, even her panting breath, into the train's wake.

Her boots sink deep, the snow turning slick under her weight and she trips. Her hands burn with the dry cold through her threadbare gloves as she pushes herself back to her feet. The light has gone out in the kitchen, the curtain upstairs is still, and Marie-Eve stumbles to the tracks, skidding up the raised bank until she stands between the rails, looking north. There is no sound, but a vibration shudders up through the soles of her boots, a rhythm like distant iron wheels on steel rails.

She might have stood there all night if the milk truck hadn't clattered around the curve, and an absurd fear of being caught in its headlights' beams sends her scrambling back to the house.

Papa sells the last of the cows after Maman dies. The corn stalks after harvest stubble the field, waiting to be plowed under in the spring. Marie-Eve cooks, and makes the long drive to town when the old truck doesn't freeze up and when the roads aren't iced. She thinks, more than once, about driving away for good, but Papa stays, and she can't leave him alone. And in some part of her mind, she cannot imagine leaving the house. If she leaves, she sometimes thinks when she's lying in the dark listening to the frost creep across the walls, then the house will somehow cease to exist.

Or perhaps she will cease to exist anywhere but the house.

One night, the winter after she takes Papa to the hospital in Chicoutimi for the last time, Marie-Eve hears a sound like the barn door banging on its hinges. The only thing inside it now is the plow the farmer who leases the land has stored there until spring comes, but she pulls on Papa's old coat anyway. Her boots creak into the cornflour-dry snow and her breath steams with every stabbing-cold breath. She shoves her hands deep in her pockets and trudges out, across the tracks.

The light stabs out of the south and the ground trembles as she steps into the green-gold pool of the light at the crossing. Marie-Eve turns, because now she hears the high, keening whistle of a locomotive cutting through the night air. The black engine slices past, pushing the darkness aside like a plough turning earth. The wheels shrill with the brakes as the train rolls to a stop before her and Marie-Eve looks up at the platform between the first car and the engine. The figure in the cab turns back towards her, and through the glass of the door she sees that it is shadow on shadow. Within the cars behind it are more shadows, she can feel the weight of them moving and pressing the train on to the north. Marie-Eve looks, but the mountains are shadows, too, black on black horizon.

When she turns back, she can see the house between the train cars. A curtain at an upstairs window stirs. The greasy gold light of the lamp goes out in the kitchen. Behind her, she hears the clank of the bucket as it's dropped in the snow.

The train's wheels start to turn, and Marie-Eve hears a rattle of a truck in a distance.

Marie-Eve reaches for the platform, stepping up, falling forward into blackness as the train lurches towards the mountains.

Marie-Eve stands on the tracks, staring at the Laurentians looming on the horizon. She wonders if she could walk along the tracks and someday reach the mountains, or if they would always stay just ahead on the horizon.

Or would she be struck by a train?

She has never seen a train, but Papa says they came, once.

Maman calls from the porch. It's getting dark and the cold is crackling across the ground, so sharp Marie-Eve thinks she can hear it. There is a faint tremor in the rails, but Maman says the trains never come any more.

It is winter. It is always winter.

QUEEN of SWORDS.

The Bremen Job

~ Linda McMullen

My scarlet cloak—with its mythic riding hood—hung abstractedly on its peg, while I pondered a curious communication deposited beneath the doorframe in the hours between twilight and dawn. The embossed, snow-white envelope bore only my name: *Poppy*.

I heard my mother stirring, chirruping at the birds, just as always. Soon she would stoke the ebon coals and knead her day away, preparing the inevitable loaves that I would take to my grandmother's table. I stole outside, borrowing the robins' perch on a stump just outside. I could not bear to break the seal—a crimson tome, with a double-pointed oval superimposed over its pages. I lifted it carefully from the envelope and extracted my letter like a thief, or a magician.

Dear Poppy,

We would like to extend to you an invitation to join our organization, and to obtain the duties and privileges thereof, for our mutual benefit. If you wish to attend today's gathering, please present yourself at a quarter to ten at the wishing well.

Our representative will look for your red cloak.
Sincerely,

The FTH Society

Persuading my mother to allow me to gather wildflowers while she baked and swept and washed required all
the childlike charm I could boast—no simple matter for
a girl teetering on the precipice of womanhood. Particularly as I had spent much of the previous day lost in my
book of wildflowers. But I promised to gather dandeli-
ons for a salad too, tipping the balance. "My indulgence
will prove your undoing," she sighed. I kissed her and
skipped away.

The village well appeared deserted when I arrived. I
had neglected to bring a pail, so the villagers eyed me
with the self-congratulating scorn of a priggish priest
hearing extravagant confessions. I rinsed the dust from
my hands, for the sake of appearing to do something—
and then a movement caught my eye.

A slim young woman gestured from the shadow of the
church—

But it seemed that only her pale forearm emerged from
the darkness . . .

I followed.

She turned southward without acknowledging my
inquisitive footfalls, or even tilting her head—with its
heavy crown of auburn hair—toward me. She kept her
arms crossed before her as we passed into the forest,

and we marched on, on, until she suddenly descended into a cleft in the ground, tracing a gumdrop-mushroom path I had never glimpsed before. The breeze tickled me with hints of cinnamon and clove. The spruce and oaks grew denser; the air grew closer; we came to a cottage half-concealed in the undergrowth—

A magnificent gingerbread structure, next to a tiny, flowing creek.

I followed the girl to the sugar-glass door; she opened it wide but remained on the threshold, barring my entry. She finally turned and I saw, for certain, that she had no hands. "Turn out your cloak and hood, and open your basket." As I did so, she stood aside, so that the many wide eyes within could see; I could feel their suddenly undammed curiosity flowing over me.

"You may enter," called a melodious voice from within.

I obeyed, only to discover that the sweetly beautiful cottage was thoroughly bewitched: what seemed like a residence for perhaps one sweet-toothed misanthrope magically allowed dozens of damsels to fit comfortably. They reclined on marzipan divans and lemon drop cushions and a sugar plum sofa. I did my best to curtsey.

"Yes," murmured the ageless sage enthroned on a fairy-food pedestal, "I see it." Turning to me, she said, "Have a seat, Poppy."

"I'll just . . . dust off this stool," said a young woman I recognized as Cinderella, retrieving one from a closet.

"That one is too hard," complained a girl with bouncy flaxen curls.

"It's fine," I said, thanking Cinderella.

"Excellent," said the wise woman. "Welcome, ladies, to this meeting of the Fairy Tale Heroines Society." I could have sworn she vouchsafed me a wink. "Our younger generation has finally come of age, so I am pleased to introduce to you three potential new members: Poppy with her red riding hood"—I waved—"Goldilocks"—my complaining, curly-haired companion smiled—"and Gretel, whom I would like to thank for hosting us all today." A round-faced, doughty girl bowed her head in acknowledgement.

"I'm so sorry," interrupted the young woman with the siren's voice, as she sank onto the arm of the sofa, accidentally jostling Cinderella. "I feel as though I've been walking on knives all day." (I learned later that walking hurt her greatly; she made herself useful by doing much of the cooking, though she flatly refused to prepare seafood.)

The wise woman arched her brow. "Ladies," she said, gesturing to Goldilocks, Gretel, and myself, "Joining the society means divorcing yourself from the lives you've known, the habits you've developed, the stories you've told. It means commitment to this group above all, and unswerving obedience to our mission—"

"What's your mission?" interjected Goldilocks.

"—which is to address our broken relationships with Grimm, and Perrault, and Hans Christian Andersen," continued the wise woman, as if there had been no interruption.

"And Robert Southey?" Goldilocks broke in. The wise woman stared at her until Goldilocks flushed and looked down at her shoes, which were undoubtedly too small.

"I suppose," conceded the wise woman, looking as though she was reconsidering the wisdom of her own invitation decisions. "Well. Girls. Yes or no?"

Gretel waved, which I supposed meant yes. Goldilocks said, "I have too little information—"

"Too bad," said the wise woman. "Poppy?"

"Wait!" cried Goldilocks. "I . . . didn't mean . . . that is . . . I . . . I'll join."

"Poppy?" the wise woman said again.

"Yes, ma'am," I said.

We took our vows of allegiance. The girl with six brothers rose with a swanlike grace to get beverages, while my friend with no hands picked up a massive bowl of pears and offered them around. Then the *real* meeting began.

"The plan, ladies," declared the wise woman, "is that we're going to break into the Repository at Bremen."

The phlegmatic Gretel didn't bat an eye, but Goldilocks gasped and I couldn't help feeling slightly taken aback. The Repository was the archive. The source of the source texts. The Official Tellings of all our tales, sanctified by the authors themselves.

"You're mad," Goldilocks declared. "Those stories are sacred! The authors have placed them under layers of protection to keep anyone—including us—from tampering with them! I've heard they're under incredibly heavy guard!"

"Do you wish to rescind your participation?" the wise woman asked, drawing out her wand and extending it toward Goldilocks's trademark hair, adding, "I can make it look permanently ratted, you know."

Goldilocks gulped and muttered a shamefaced apology.

"Now, we exist only as marionettes," intoned the wise woman. "We follow the pre-trod paths, day in, day out—without ever having lived a day in our lives. Or even seen our own scripts. Well, no more!" she cried. "We are going to reclaim those texts. And we are going to create something better in their wake. We are finished playing the parts that men wrote for us!"

Applause; determined, almost grim, expressions.

"Thanks to our very own goose girl, who has been lingering with her flock outside the Repository for the last several weeks, we have excellent information about external security. The Repository boasts two guards outside its entrance at all times. They work eight-hour shifts. We know that at least five of these guards are susceptible to some kind of temptation, but one of them is extremely brave, absolutely impervious to shivers of any kind. We will therefore schedule our infiltration around his shift."

Cinderella went about collecting the pear cores. "Sorry. Habit."

The wise woman sighed and continued. "Allerleirauh will be in charge of disguises," she began. "Then Inge—" she gestured to my handless guide—"will conduct the team through the forest; she's spent an extensive amount of time in there, mapping the route. Once you arrive, Plan A is that Eva"—she gestured to a pretty, pouty young woman—"will arrive just before the end of the midnight-to-dawn shift with soup to offer the hungry guards. Obviously, it will contain donkey cabbage, which will literally transform the guards into the braying asses they are. In the unlikely event that they refuse free food, plan B is to have Snow White lure them into the woods. The dwarves have generously rented their cottage to us, and she's booby-trapped it to a nicety."

"What if only one of them goes?" I asked.

"Gretel's more than a match for any one of them," the wise woman replied. "She took out a witch when she was underfed and terrified, and she's been in training since then."

Gretel flexed her biceps.

"Indeed. And we'll be sending additional support. At any rate, once our team enters the repository, they will have to work through the information warren inside. Goldilocks, I understand, has some experience with housebreaking, so I'll ask her to take the lead on devising a plan to navigate through the building. Our goal is to reach the safe, which is located on the third floor, in the very center of the building."

"Of course it is," Goldilocks muttered, but accepted the blueprint the wise woman handed her.

"We expect that Sleeping Beauty will be able to pick the lock with her spindle—*stop playing with that, dear!*" cried the wise woman, as the princess let her fingertips dance a hair's-breadth over its lethal-looking point. "If that doesn't work, our fisherman's wife has a range of hooks available." An ill-at-ease peasant woman nodded from the corner. "Then—"

Beauty waved from the corner.

"That's right. The strike team will extract the original texts of all our tales, and bring them back here for Beauty to analyze. Then we'll make decisions about what to do. Cinderella will also remain at headquarters with me; she'll look after anyone who gets injured. Understood?"

"How can I help?" I asked. My voice sounded very small. I didn't have any magical powers, or exceptional beauty, or an enigmatic voice, or—

The wise woman smiled. "I daresay we'll find some use for you."

Day after day I told my mother I was off to visit my grandmother, while I trained with Gretel and the rest of the strike team—those the wise woman had assigned duties, plus Rapunzel, the Snow Queen (recently reclaimed from villainy through a little Disneyesque magic), a kind young woman named Clara who the wise woman explained had come straight from the three little men in the wood, and a bored young princess perpetually toying with a golden ball. We participated in physical training, conducted drills, and ran simulations. "You must be prepared," said the wise woman. "I can only foresee so much."

"Aren't there kind of a lot of us?" asked Goldilocks.

"Redundancy ensures success," replied the wise woman.

And at last, the great day arrived. The girl with the seven brothers had spun and woven, and made disguises following Allerleirauh's designs. Allerleirauh disguised Gretel, Sleeping Beauty, the Snow Queen, Golden Ball girl, the kind young woman, Rapunzel, and the fisherman's wife as security guards, tucking Rapunzel's hair into a basket on her back, and pulling her hat down as far as possible. The donkey cabbage proprietress was also dressed as a guard, with a blue cloak to conceal it. Snow White, Goldilocks and I alone remained in normal clothing, though she braided our hair and accessorized us with spectacles and satchels (she allowed me to keep my basket). "This way, you'll look like students," she said, "and you won't attract attention if you're poking around—as if looking for a book."

We made our way stealthily toward the repository, keeping to the forest as much as possible. But, true to form, I couldn't help leaving the path for some exquisite, poisonously-blue buds blooming in the glade . . .

"Really?" demanded Gretel.

"You were sent to fulfill your mission, I was sent to complete mine," I muttered, but only after she was striding forward, and well out of earshot.

The donkey cabbage plan worked like a . . . well, it was under a charm, but it's probably a bit too on-the-nose to say . . . anyway, our plans did not miscarry. Eva-the-donkey-cabbage-proprietress dragged the guards out of sight and secured them with some rope, then abandoned her cloak and returned to the front door with Inge to take their places and deflect the questions of the oncoming crew. The rest of us entered the Repository of Lore, our security "squad" marching in formation as if conducting an extra patrol. And saw, just ahead a pair of guards conducting their real duties . . .

"Go!" hissed Gretel; Snow White, Goldilocks and I dispersed into the bowels of the labyrinth, while our security team tangled noisily with the guards. I peered out from behind the multicolored array of Lang titles, lightly dusted in their rainbow jackets, anticipating pandemonium . . .

"Gentlemen!" cried the young woman who had visited the three little men of the woods, "let my colleagues be!"

With this, five gold coins fell out of her mouth. The guards withdrew their molestation-poised hands and dove for the money. A gleam danced behind her eyes; she darted back out the door, singing, dropping coins with every word, the guards in greedy pursuit.

"Two down," cried Goldilocks, delightedly, from somewhere in the stacks.

"More friends coming to join us," muttered Gretel, as another pair of guards had become aware of their colleagues' conspicuous absence. They approached, glowering, until Snow White ran up to one of them and whispered something in his ear. His face flushed, and his eyes glowed like stars. Then she whispered something in his partner's ear. A moment later she had linked arms with them both and they walked merrily out the front door. I heard her murmur, "My cabin is only a quarter-hour's walk from here . . . "

I made my way back to the security team, now smaller by two. "Will she be all right?"

"I wouldn't worry," said Gretel. "She designed the set-up, and the wise woman helped her test it. And she has plenty of experience dealing with people targeting her."

Not altogether reassured, I rejoined the others. Goldilocks navigated us through the library, carefully skirting the witches' lore section, and reminding us all to jump the enchanted stream flowing through the middle of the Bewitchment section. Universally graceful, we soared over the waters and were proceeding to the rear stairwells to reach the second—and ultimately, third floors—when Gretel held up a silent hand.

A giant stood before us, wielding a club, ready to strike.

"Any ideas?" muttered Goldilocks, out of the corner of her mouth. "Anyone?"

"Scatter!" cried Gretel, as the club came down in our midst. I dove right, landing on top of Gretel, as the giant swung his club wildly about, no doubt hoping to smash us. But we were tiny and moving fast, and in his frustration, he lifted the club and bashed against the nearest objects, which happened to be the wooden staircases. They collapsed into a heap of kindling.

"Oh, no," someone moaned.

"Help me! What have you got, girl?" cried Gretel, shaking my shoulder. I rummaged in my basket and produced the bottle of wine. She rolled her eyes, but accepted it, and ran out to face the danger. "Oi! You're nothing but an overgrown troll!" she cried. The giant, caring for neither her remark nor her tone, tried to demolish her with his club; Gretel caught it on the upswing, then leapt from it to his shoulder, whence she smashed the wine bottle over his head. As he staggered forward from the blow, he grabbed Gretel around the waist and flung her against the Anthropomorphic Items collection. She did not stir.

Goldilocks appeared out of nowhere, staring down the concussed giant and stamping her foot. "*Somebody*," she screeched, "*has been interfering with my team!*"

And she screamed aloud, the same shriek that must have given those bears infinite pause, and the giant hove himself forward, trying to smash her, trying to stop the horrible noise—and Goldilocks, displaying an impressive presence of mind, paused only to blow him him a raspberry, then, still screaming, skipped just ahead of him toward the library entrance, drawing him off . . .

"Not bad for a complaining little housebreaker," observed Gretel.

"How're we going to reach the archive?" Golden Ball girl complained. "The steps are gone, and Goldilocks's blueprint only showed the one set."

"Not very prudent of the designers, really," observed the fisherman's wife. "If I had that kind of power –"

"Focus, please," said Gretel. "Ideas, team?"

Rapunzel grinned. "Not to worry," she said, and looped

her hair over the existing bit of bannister, two stories up. She turned to me. "Poppy, you're lightest, you go first, and we'll see if this will even work."

"Great," said Gretel, standing at attention to keep Rapunzel safe.

I half-clambered up her hair as she and the rest of the team helped hoist me to the next level—then Sleeping Beauty, the fisherman's wife, Golden Ball girl, and the Snow Queen followed. Gretel and Rapunzel remained below to fend off anyone attempting to reach us from behind—"I'm certain they have enchanted ropes or ladders about for just such an emergency," she said, grimly.

Up on the third floor now, our remainder stole down a corridor, which ended in a locked door. "I've got it," cried Sleeping Beauty merrily, twirling her spindle around her thumb with an altogether worrying degree of swagger. She used the spindle's lethal tip to blindly perform the delicate mechanical surgery that would open the lock—

A *pop!* and the handle turned. Sleeping Beauty looped her prize tool around her thumb in preparation for holstering it, when it caught her on the forefinger and she slumped to the ground, unconscious.

"I don't *believe* this," cried Golden Ball girl, unfortunately catching the attention of the guard stationed just beyond the door. He seemed to weigh the situation, then took a deep breath, in preparation for issuing a monumental bellow, to let his fellows know he had found us—

But Golden Ball girl lunged forward, looping her arm around his neck, and kissing him full on the mouth. For a moment, I couldn't distinguish anything through a cloud of acrid green smoke, and then, I saw—

—a frog emerging from the depths of the guard's crumpled uniform.

"*That's* your power?" I cried.

She shrugged. "Supposedly I can also change an upstanding, enchanted frog into a prince, but good luck finding one of those. So far, the magic only cuts this way."

"Break in now, meta-analysis later!" cried the Snow Queen. "Mathilde"—she gestured to our resident faunamorphosis expert—"You've done your bit, look after Sleeping Beauty." She transformed the corridor behind us into ice, and erected an ice slide down to the lower level.

"You couldn't have just made us an ice ladder back there?" Mathilde replied, earning her a withering glance from the Snow Queen. Mathilde—I imagined, partly to escape from the remainder of this conversation—asked to borrow my cloak, and I obliged; we helped her place Sleeping Beauty on top of it, and Mathilde dragged our fallen comrade carefully back to the rest of the team on the makeshift stretcher/toboggan.

And the rest of us crept onward, coming across another locked door. The fisherman's wife fileted the lock; it clattered onto the floor and I half-imagined smoke and whimpers emerging from it.

"Excellent," said the Snow Queen.

Then the lights went out.

The Snow Queen, the fisherman's wife, and I crept forward, when we heard a short scream suddenly cut off—then silence.

Our picklock turned tail and ran back toward the rest of the team, and the light . . .

"Do your ice powers also extend to—"

"No," she said. "Do you have anything useful in your basket?"

I shook my head, ruefully, painfully conscious of the fact that my sole contribution to that point had been attendance.

The Snow Queen sighed.

The light flickered on beyond the cracked door.

And then, an inhuman voice:

"Come and play, Red . . . "

I trembled from my red riding hood to my little boots, a primal, wordless terror surging through me—

The Snow Queen murmured, "I'm right beside you. We'll go together."

I nodded, and—with every ounce of my will focused on my leaden feet—stumbled forward through the door, whose plaque read: *The Dorothea Viehmann Repository.*

We came into the room, the frozen heart of the archive, a dim, windowless, box-shaped room lined with iron caskets, locked drawers and stout safes—

—and before them prowled The Wolf.

I forced the scream fighting for exit back down my constricted throat. He was savage and sensual, with talons that beckoned even as they threatened to rip me apart . . . and what big eyes he had—hypnotic yellow discs . . .

"I hope you've come to play," he said, his eyes flickering from me to the Snow Queen and back again. My fingers snaked into my basket, hoping by some miracle that the wise woman would choose now to work a miracle, to deliver me a weapon that appeared just from wishing—but I found nothing but the bread and the flowers. I offered him the former, gripping the flowers, as if their cheerful color might offer some comfort.

"I'm hungry, all right," he returned, "but not for bread. Still, I'll keep it. The better to eat you with."

And then he *lunged* at us. The Snow Queen, anticipating his attack, threw up an ice wall between him and us, but he powered through it, sending both of us flying, and dispersing ice shards into every corner of the room . . . I struggled to right myself, only to find her grappling with him, hand to hand, his torrid breath scorching her face . . . But he was in no hurry, always preferring to play with his food before he finally ate it—

"Poppy!" she gasped, his fangs grazing her throat.

And time seemed to slow, to lose all meaning, and of all things, my wildflower book seemed to dance before my eyes, and I remembered I had seen a picture of those beautiful blue flowers in my basket, several days before, on the page . . .

Aconitum, also known as aconite, or monkshood, also possesses the curious nickname of wolf's bane . . .

I seized an ice shard from the floor, squeezed a few drops of the flowers' venomous nectar onto its tip, and plunged it into the wolf's broad back.

He howled in surprise and misery and pain—and then the tremors began; he rolled off the Snow Queen and onto his side, spewing expletives and curses that ended with: " . . . Red."

Then he moved no more.

I rushed to the Snow Queen: "Are you all right?"

"Fine," she replied, wearily; she had a great lump on her head from where she had hit it in her fall. "Go find which strongbox our files are in, will you?"

I did as she bid, deciphering the faded ink scrawls on tiny labels affixed to the safes and drawers. After examining several—*British Nursery Rhymes*, *Folklore: West Africa*, *Chivalric Tales*, and so on—I came to a pot-bellied safe whose label read: *Fairy Tales, Original Versions*. I pointed. The Snow Queen propped herself up, and sent a wave of ice and snow around it. Her magic swirled, dropping the temperature of the room so abruptly that my teeth began to chatter . . . and then—to my astonishment—the safe shattered.

The Snow Queen tumbled senseless to the floor.

"No!" I shouted, but a little voice inside reminded me not to allow her to have struggled in vain. I began picking through the silvery slivers of the former safe, extracting sheaves of carefully ribbon-bound, yellowing papers, and storing them in my basket. Footsteps sounded in the hall; I picked up another ice shard that felt friendly in my hand, and waited, crouched defensively—

"Thank God!" exclaimed Gretel, pulling me into an unexpected and slightly bone-crushing hug. "You're alive!

We thought—" She finally spotted the Snow Queen on the floor, bent down over her with careful fingers on her neck. "She's alive. I'll carry her. You've got the stories?"

I nodded because speech would not come. Gretel threw the meager royal weight across her shoulders, and said, "Let's get out of here."

Golden Ball girl—Mathilde, I mean—had clearly re-connected with the rest of the team; leaving Rapunzel to care for Sleeping Beauty, she had gone about kissing all of the remaining guards. The only thing that slowed our exit was trying to avoid stepping on the phalanx of frogs.

Back at the little cottage, Cinderella had put most of the injured to rights. The Snow Queen rested on the sofa, lifting a hand to her still-tender head, but smiling. Gretel and the rest of the security crew had suffered numerous contusions, and many of them had ice on their injuries. Poor Rapunzel had an awful headache from everyone pulling on her hair, and she had a blindfold on and an ice pack on her head, but she was humming a merry tune. The kind young woman who produced coins when she spoke had led the guards pursuing her to Snow White's cottage, where they—like the two invited by Snow White—had gotten snared in the various traps. The two of them were only sore from running, and lounged in adjacent armchairs.

Goldilocks and I remained well, albeit rattled.

Unfortunately, however, neither Cinderella nor the wise woman had yet discovered a cure for Sleeping Beauty. She had perused the ancient text, of course, and found that the *official* story prescribed a prince . . . She had nonetheless tried to work other spells. Not one of them had made the least difference, and our companion slumbered on.

While she did so, the wise woman came to me, and clasped both my hands in hers. "Poppy, we owe you our thanks. You faced a particularly personal battle, and emerged triumphant. I am so appreciative—and, if I may say so, I am very proud of you."

I blushed as red as my hood. "I—thank you, but I am just so sorry so many of our sisters got injured—"

"They accepted that risk, just as you did," the wise woman replied. "I just wish I were sagacious enough to—" She frowned at herself, glancing toward Sleeping Beauty.

Shaking her head in bewilderment, the wise woman convened those present, and gave Beauty the floor. Beauty went on at some length, describing the individual stories to gasps and frowns. She had just finished "The Three Little Men in the Wood" and we were enjoying a break when Mathilde jumped up and cried, "Where's Clara?"

"Gathering strawberries, why?"

"We need her! Which way did she go?"

The wise woman looked frankly bewildered. "West, I think."

"Great!" cried Mathilde, over her shoulder, as she bolted out the door. We all stared after her in bewilderment.

Beauty cleared her throat, gently, and resumed her narrations. When she had read all of our stories, she said, "I've gone through these tales several times." She pursed her lips. "Most of them appear to have been written to caution girls –" She glanced toward me—"against straying from the path—or, in my own case, for example, to teach young women to accept their fates with grace . . . and docility." She frowned. "But in my view, these lessons belong to another age—"

At that moment, Mathilde and Clara returned with a third, blindfolded young woman, a stranger, and Mathilde's expression was triumphant. "Sorry to interrupt," she said, "but I've had an idea."

"Bringing unapproved strangers here?" demanded the wise woman.

"She can't see anything," pointed out Mathilde. "But I think we need her . . . "

"For what?"

"Curing Sleeping Beauty," continued Mathilde.

Clara broke in, apologetically. "This is my stepsister. When I went to the house in the wood, the three little men put a charm on me, that makes me drop coins from my mouth when I speak—" By the end of this explanation, she had produced enough gold to fund the Society for a year. "But my stepsister—ah . . . "

"She was cursed with toads jumping out of her mouth at every word," Mathilde explained. "So, I thought if I could just get my hands . . . or, rather, my mouth on *one* magical toad . . . "

"I thought your magic worked on *frogs*?" asked the wise woman, sharply.

"I thought it close enough to merit an *attempt*," Mathilde retorted. "It can't hurt. Go on, Bertha."

Bertha hissed, "No!" but it was enough; a gruesome amphibian sprang from her lips. Mathilde scooped him up and kissed him . . .

. . . a puff of gold-and-plum smoke—

—and a beautiful, slightly vacant-eyed prince appeared, looking dazed. "My savior!" he cried, lurching amorously toward Mathilde—

"Not me," she replied, promptly. "I did it on her behalf," she said, pointing toward Sleeping Beauty. The prince, uncomprehending but amenable, kissed Sleeping Beauty full on the lips. She stirred prettily, blinked, and murmured, "What did I miss?"

The prince cried, "My love!" and Sleeping Beauty wrinkled her forehead and frowned at him, and Mathilde came to the rescue and kissed him so that he turned back into a toad. Then she carried him carefully out to the creek and wished him good luck. Clara sent her stepsister off with some coins.

"There is a certain elegance in the original tales' simplicity," Beauty continued, as if there had been no interruption. "But they offer us no agency." She glanced toward the wise woman, who dipped her chin affirmatively.

"Therefore," she said, "I propose that we produce our own versions of the tales—where we women *act*, and *choose*, and *live*."

Mathilde began a slow clap, and then Rapunzel joined, and soon the whole room dissolved in thunderous applause.

"There's just one . . . small concern, however," said Beauty. "Once we've written our new editions, we'll need to—somehow—place them inside the archive . . . "

Jamón Íberico

~ *Lexi Pérez*

Every moment of our ancestry has culminated in the DNA coding—the *programming*—of our minds, bodies, and souls. We have a prime directive: survive and procreate. We are driven by our programming. We are our programming.

There's this pig. This kind of pig that only eats acorns from some specific place for its whole life. This strict diet creates a marbling of the pig's fat and muscle that, when dry-aged, makes for some very expensive ham. *Jamón Íberico*.

Jamón Íberico is served everywhere in Spain, and it's easily identified wherever you find it because it's the only kind of meat served straight from the corpse.

This is only a minor exaggeration, as the meat is dry-aged by the leg. Restaurants and merchants buy legs of ham at a time, and cut strips of flesh so thin you can nearly see through it. Even then, shaving it slice by slice, they must sell it for an exorbitant price, to make up for the massive upfront cost of an entire damn pig leg.

The first time I saw *Jamón Íberico*, I didn't recognize it for what it was. I didn't recognize it at all. I was with my mother, young, maybe ten, maybe eleven, and I saw something dense and heavy and oblong set proudly on display on the bartop. I remember creeping closer and closer, finding a smell, being unable to place the smell, creeping closer. I remember staring—squinting—at the prickly spikes of wiry fur left around the bony ankle, tracing my eyes up and down the shining metal of the stand. It wasn't until my mother's confused and displeased hand fell upon my shoulder that I saw, with horror, the thing I was actually looking at.

A shackle was strapped around the ankle of the pig. The hoof, still dirty, pointed haphazardly to the far right corner of the restaurant. It was presented so prominently, so proudly; the curved metal arm that held the cuff high glinted malevolently, and the mahogany base shone. A wire, like a potter might use on his clay, lay draped over the exposed meat of the creature's thigh. As I watched, stupefied, enamored, a hand drew the wire up the pink, white, and tan leg - a parchment thin sheaf of ham curling behind it. The smell, still unrecognizable, slapped me across the nose again, before encasing me, seeping into my hair. I decided it must be the smell of being buried alive.

The most striking thing about first seeing *Jamón Ibérico* is how easily such a cuff would fit around your ankle, how similar in length they might be, toe to thigh. From time to time, I will catch a glimpse of myself, in some such position, and see immediately, for a moment or a glance, exactly how like *Jamón Ibérico* my leg could look. Some of these times, when I close my eyes, I can see the thin little wire, stroking up my thigh, up again and again and to the bone, leaflets of ham fluttering away.

Strip by bloodless strip.

Thin enough to see through.

Just one leg lasts ages. Ages and ages.

I've always been proud of my physique. Particularly my legs. Not proud in a sense where I needed to show them off. Just proud in the sense that my legs were strong, and powerful, and would never let me down. The cut of the calf was deep; flexing them, I saw the thickness of the muscle, knew it could do whatever I asked. The cut of each thigh, while less pronounced, was no less impressive. My legs were heavy. Dense. *Strong.*

There was a man in Germany who posted an ad on Craigslist, asking if anyone would be interested in eating him alive. Another man responded, saying yes, yes he would like to eat that man alive. The two got together and wrote up a contract. The contract detailed the sequence of events that would transpire, and that they each recognized the potential repercussions of such events. They both signed it.

The first thing the second man did was cut the penis from the first man, and fry it. I don't remember if they both ate that or not, but at a certain point, does it even matter? The second man was arrested, but as he had that contract, they had to let him walk. There was no law against cannibalism in Germany at the time.

There is now.

I've heard human flesh tastes like pork. I've heard it's the only other kind of meat that would. I've heard reasoning for these claims, but I don't remember any of it. I know there is an illness that can be contracted from cannibalism, but I also know this only comes from eating the brain.

All living creatures, regardless of intellect or wisdom or willpower, are simple reproductions of their programming, as adapted to the circumstances they arrived in. It was never nature versus nurture, only nature and nurture—only us.

It is our nature to protect ourselves, propagate ourselves, to perpetuate the self. Any action taken contrary to this nature, this directive, is contrary to our programming. To attack one's own flesh, in the animal world, is a sign of intense sickness, parasitic and contrary in nature to the very being of the animal itself. In the human world, too, the act often indicates sickness of the mind, or (and) a product of religion. It is not impossible for us to break from our programming, it is just very difficult to do so. Someone who inherited OCD, who has it locked in their genetic coding, who has to touch every wall in the room six times before they can leave it, will tell you very quickly that this genetic quirk of their pro-gramming does not promote either their survival or pro-creation, though every bit of their nature screams that not to do it is to die. Yet, with much work, much labor, much hardship - through therapy, and medication, and practice—this person can slowly disentangle themselves —their true selves - from this programming.

But what does consuming the self do? You are both destroying and preserving the very thing evolution has taught it to protect.

There was a man who rode a motorcycle. He got in an accident. His leg, separated from his body in the crash, was impossible to reattach. As his leg was his property, he brought it home. He called his friends. They had a barbecue.

In some ways—many ways—I envy this man.

He did it the easy way.

I've read about so many accounts of autocannibalism in humans. Almost all of them were forced. Prisoners of war forced to eat their own ears, men on drugs biting off their own fingers and swallowing them - even the man on the motorcycle didn't truly choose to eat himself, he simply ate a piece of meat that *used* to be himself.

☉

I have gotten a lot of sympathy since the accident. The trauma to my body impacted my mind, and this was quickly noticed by those around me. I, in turn, noticed their noticing. I sent everyone away, told them I needed to heal.

In reality, it had just gotten too hard to fit in anymore. Too hard to smile at the right time or make the right joke. It wasn't just the pain, not just the stress, it was also the tantalizing distraction of anticipation. The energy of my mind could hardly be spent on mundane pleasantries—no matter how well-meaning my visitors were.

Prosthetics are better than they've ever been. Thanks to kind donations and my own comfortable savings, I have one for everyday wear—walking, sitting, driving, etc - one for hiking, and one for swimming.

Yes, it does have a flipper.

You don't actually walk on a fake leg—you more sit on it. My nub doesn't take any of my weight, it just has a nice little cup to lean back in.

I didn't host a barbecue, if that's what you're thinking. I might, eventually. But *Jamón Íberico* is dry-aged, not cooked.

Even though I know it's not nearly time yet, I limp out to the backyard, hobble over to the shed. I already know what to expect when I open the door, but the smell still surprises me—it smells like being buried alive.

In the Night Forest

~ *Tori Fredrick*

In 1984, she told her fourth-grade class that she was a test tube baby and had no sense of smell. In sixth grade, she told two of her closest friends that she was from a secret lineage of witches and had already said too much. In ninth grade, she told her first boyfriend that her father was part of a pedophile ring and had forced her to do awful things. Only one of these things was true, although she didn't know it at the time.

Dinner was served in the dining room, and Rachel dreaded the evening round of conversation that circled without her, Whitney and her mother on the same side of the table, laughing together and making the same gestures, like acolytes in the same church. They looked more like sisters than mother and daughter and Rachel burned with envy. She suspected that abundance was a myth. Whitney drew things into her own orbit, her eyes like dark planets sparkling, leaving no room for other suns. Rachel thought sometimes about melting away her sister's face and features with acid or a blowtorch, leaving her monstrous but with her hands and vision unaffected so that she could still do her precious art.

"We have a special occasion," her father said, the shadows of his face accented, cross-sectioned between the chandelier above and the candles flickering from the table below. Whitney pushed her glass forward to be filled with wine, her father standing like a dark sentinel, ready to pour. Rachel knew the special occasion was not hers, and they were in full "art school scouting" mode for Whitney, so the announcement of not one but two scholarship offers did not surprise her, as Whitney was something of a prodigy.

She pulled her own half-filled glass of wine back to her plate, and tried to smile, but it was so hard. Her expression must have betrayed something, because her mother said, "Can't you ever just be happy for somebody else?" cheeks pink, and her eyes . . . her eyes like pebbles thrown against Rachel's face, stinging in their regard. "What have we said about the attitude?"

Whitney made a face over her mother's shoulder, shrugging a little. "Mom . . ." she said, her voice persuasive, soft, and Rachel's eyes flooded with sudden tears, grateful.

"She knows what she's doing," their mother said, but waved a hand in dismissal and raised her glass for a toast.

There was a family rule, designed for her, about sullenness at dinner—she was to leave it on the sideboard before sitting down. It only made her angrier when they called her out on things. She didn't know if they understood just how angry she could become.

☉

Rachel thought of her life as the ugly duckling story in reverse. Her father took a series of photos of her as a toddler, playing with a bouquet of flowers bought just for her, all golden curls and smiles. She found the photo book in his desk and didn't recognize herself at first—she seldom smiled now, and her eyes in these pictures were large and luminous, more like Whitney's than her own, which were small now and set close to her broad, pasty nose. She tried to fix her tiny eyes with promised remedies from stolen drugstore magazines, filled with teenage girl stuff that she wouldn't want anybody to catch her looking at, because she could imagine people wondering why would she even bother? She lost the golden hair in kindergarten, when it turned straight and slack and became almost no color at all—like dishwater runoff. She dyed it black now, to match her eyeliner and dark lipstick, echoing a growing trend, although she didn't know it.

Rachel had lost other things over the years, too. She was good at math for a nanosecond, in elementary school. She remembered even now her heart swelling with a stuttering excitement when they selected her for the gifted program, and her father was so proud when he heard. She decided maybe smart was better than pretty.

Rachel's father, a neuroscientist who taught at the university, was usually detached from the household drama, which made his attention to her during this time especially noteworthy.

He started her on violin lessons, buying her a tiny silver instrument for her charm bracelet, explaining that the neural centers for skill in math and music were correlated.

"Music is math," he told her.

Rachel's mother protested at her choice of instrument, claiming that an untrained violin player was perhaps worse than almost anything. But Rachel had been good, at first. It was during this time that Whitney experienced some unexpected setbacks in her middle school algebra course, which she had been encouraged to take early. It was unusual even then for Whitney to have problems with anything, and the feeling of surpassing her sister in any way was one Rachel would not experience again during their childhood.

Rachel remembered the night when she thought it must have happened. She awoke in her room, a round moon streaming light through opalescent curtain sheers, her head pounding but unable to move her body, her limbs feeling thick and grotesquely proportioned, as though she were a wad of clay, heavy and wet. She fell back asleep eventually, but when she awoke the next morning, something was different.

She got ready for school as usual, but her head still hurt a little, and when she got to her special math class her mind felt foggy and stuck.

"How can you multiply a negative number times a negative number and get a positive?" she asked her teacher, unable to either make sense of this concept or let it go, hitting her head with her hands in frustration. They sent her to the nurse's office where her mother was called to come and get her because of her headache.

Rachel's mother made a nest for her on the couch at home from an old quilt and pillows, stroking her forehead and bringing pills which she taught Rachel how to swallow. This softness from her mother was unusual, and she remembered closing her eyes beneath the gentle hands, as though she were one of her mother's statues, being shaped from nothingness, a tattoo like an elongated star at the edge of her consciousness.

She lost the music at the same time, her fingers fat and clumsy, the violin strings cutting into her flesh but as foreign, suddenly, as a lost language. Her father ordered an MRI which was not yet common medical practice, but it revealed nothing. She lost the little charm from her bracelet but was happy and not sad that it was gone. She told the test tube lie not long after this, basing it on something she saw on the news, having no clear idea why she would say such a thing.

Rachel was the fifth girl Josh asked to the homecoming dance. Although a little dismayed when her friend Sonia told her how many other girls he asked first, Rachel didn't really hold it against him. She usually kept a running tally of as many as six or seven crushes herself; since none of them ever went anywhere anyhow, it kept things interesting to be open to multiple possibilities. She understood.

She'd known Josh since elementary school. He wasn't cute, exactly, but then her crush list did not usually include highly attractive people, because she considered herself a realist. His glasses were always a little greasy around the edges, his jeans were acid-washed and high-waisted, and he had a poorly drawn tattoo of a lizard on one ankle. When she asked him in homeroom if it was his spirit animal, he shrugged a little and said he wished he had gotten a barbecued chicken leg instead, because his current tattoo had the same degree of significance. Rachel found this hilarious and laughed so hard that he smiled a little when he looked at her, and she thought it might have been then when she was added to the bottom of his list.

When he asked her to go with him, all of his flaws folded into the wholeness of who he was, and Rachel felt a flooded warmth at her core, leaving all her practiced shrugs of indifference about boys and school dances on the cutting room floor. Faced with the unexpected need to purchase a dress, she called her grandmother, snaking the coil of the long telephone cord into the hallway bathroom for privacy. She didn't want to ask her mother for the money, and she trembled with gratitude when her grandmother suggested they could shop for it together.

Her bone-thin and dark-eyed grandmother used a cane that Rachel always thought she managed to make look like a scepter and didn't insult Rachel by suggesting that she try on dresses in any shade of pink or pastel. Although Rachel felt her usual discomfort amidst rows of gleaming merchandise and pretty clerks in the store at the mall, she appreciated this. She selected two dresses in black to try, and one in a dark fabric which looked black but had hints of red in the folds or in the light. Her grandmother did not insist that she come out and model them, as her mother would have done, and this thing which might have indicated indifference felt like kindness. Dressing room mirrors were merciless.

Her grandmother also didn't demonstrate any particular interest in conversation, and they were quiet on the drive home, Rachel's dress folded into a package with an elegance that outdid her own. At the same time, she wondered at the silence.

"Mom had a sister, right?" she asked the question without quite knowing why. The circumstances of her death were somewhat mysterious to Rachel, although she knew it involved a car accident, and wondered now if she were introducing the topic at a thoughtless time.

Her grandmother looked at Rachel sideways. "She did."

"What was she like?" Rachel didn't know if she cared, but it was never talked about, and maybe her mom's sister had been more like her, maybe there was a story that would help her make sense of her own origins. Maybe her grandmother missed this other daughter, and Rachel could fill some void.

"She was a good girl, but unhappy. Sometimes we are made that way." No emotion betrayed her grandmother's face or voice, but Rachel thought that it must be there, just masked or frozen, like petrified wood. Further discussion did not seem welcome, so Rachel subsided back into silence.

Her mother heard about the dress, of course, but let it go with a shrug of her own.

"Have fun," she said on the night of the dance, taking photos of Rachel and Josh along with Whitney and her date, urging them all not to stay out too late.

The school gym doubled as the cafeteria and smelled like a mixture of old sweat and prison food, although with the lights dimmed and disco balls rolling, a veil seemed draped over the relentlessness of daily life, and Rachel felt gratitude for the forgiving darkness. They danced, which she wasn't sure she could even do, and shivered under Josh's hands on her hips, the warmth from his palms electric. They didn't tell Whitney when they decided to leave, stumbling across the parking lot together, music fading behind the tiny rectangle of light issuing from the opened gymnasium doors, crisp leaves under their dress shoes, the football field dark beneath the night sky, the metal bleachers cold as they crawled underneath.

"We can go to my place," she whispered after their hands found each other, "we have a separate house in the back."

A friend of Josh's dropped them off down the road and Rachel pulled off her shoes before leading them in through the surrounding woods. The pool house loomed in quarry stone and aged wood as they approached, Joshua behind Rachel, both laughing, although they were trying to be quiet. She fumbled her key from a tiny clutch purse, black like her dress, the door resisting a little in its frame, both painted a classic, pristine white.

Rachel's grandmother stayed in the upstairs apartment when she visited, which remained true to the old New England roots of the building, but the downstairs was sharp and modern, displaying her mother's goddess statues, all breasts and vulvic triangles, unseeing eyes dulled to the magic of this particular moment. She turned the track lighting on for a moment before thinking better of it, illuminating a shadowy circle of figures that although often faceless seemed to be watching, nevertheless.

Josh stumbled against her when she turned out the lights, whispering around soft laughter, "Thank god, those are creepy." His breath against her neck smelled like the peach liquor and sour candy they had under the bleachers.

She reached forward and touched his face, his acne-marred skin under her fingers taut and a little chapped, occasionally scabbed, and she imagined him using astringents or other miracle cures, drying his skin but fixing nothing, and a rush of sympathy flooded her, because she understood.

She grabbed his hand again, warm and only slightly larger than hers and urged him up the narrow stairs to the apartment's living room, a braided rug warming the floor and they rolled onto the couch together, limbs tangling. She cried later without really knowing why, suspecting this moment in its sweetness could not last and would melt away under the ruthless light of day. When Josh asked her what was wrong, she said the thing about her father without truly understanding the words coming out of her mouth or why she would tell such a story, but the details of shadowy figures and brutal twisted things she was forced to do spilled forward with lives of their own, evidencing a dark imagination she didn't know she had. Josh made disbelieving sounds and held her, but the moment had devolved into strangeness and she could sense his deep discomfort and desire to escape.

On the night of Whitney's celebratory dinner, Rachel awoke in bed with a headache that might have been from the wine, since she drank as much as she thought she could get away with, then finished the second bottle in the kitchen. Unable to fall back asleep, she sat on the ledge outside her bedroom window, the moon full, the joint she just finished making her hands tremble as she smoked cigarette after cigarette. Bone-white light cast chilly shadows across the yard, lengthening like long fingers reaching for the surrounding dark. She tracked movement near the pool house and scuttled across the roof for a better view. Several figures departed the dimly lit building into the woods beyond their property, walking in silence without flashlights, anonymous in the night forest.

Rachel crawled back in through her bedroom window, the ache in her head dulled but not gone, and descended through the dark house to make her way outdoors. She crept past the rhododendrons on the back deck and skirted the edge of the pool, drained now for the season. There was no path to follow but she didn't hesitate to enter the surrounding woods and she could have sworn

she felt the presences which came before her as her feet
guided her without incident to a clearing amid a group
of silent figures.

Her vision was disturbed but she recognized her mother and Whitney, their faces coming clear then shudder-
ing away in shadows, their clothing dark and indistinct.

"What are you doing here, Rachel?" and the voice
was her grandmother's, calm but so cold, her white hair
threaded with black, and it felt like a betrayal, that her
grandmother would be here, although she couldn't have
said where "here" was in the first place.

Rachel had no words, her tongue heavy and stuck, and
then she saw it, the thing laying on a stone table like a
lump of wet clay given cursory human form. It was moving, a little, flailing arms and shaking its shapeless face
from side to side. It had rudimentary hands, but no fingers, and its head missing a chunk of what would be skull
and brain matter if it were in fact a living thing. Its eyes
were gouged out and replaced with tiny dark pebbles set
far back in the sockets. She stepped closer.

"What is this?" she asked, her voice so quiet she didn't
know if she'd spoken aloud.

"Go back to bed, Rachel," her mother said, and her
head, suddenly, was pounding again, and she wanted
more than anything to obey this voice, with its unac-
customed gentleness, and when she looked, she thought
her mother might almost be crying, and before she became afraid her heart melted at the thought that the tears
might be for her.

Rachel stepped closer to the thing on the . . . was it an altar? . . . in the center of the grove, and leaning in she saw something familiar wedged into the hole where the figure's heart might have been, and recognized the tiny violin charm her father had given her, and she wanted to snatch it back but didn't quite dare.

She reached her hand forward, and then her grandmother was there, black eyes glittering. "Rachel, this isn't happening," she said, and her voice was like metronome, inevitable, soothing. "None of us are here. This is a dream, a bad dream."

Rachel closed her eyes, because this had to be true. It wasn't the drugs, surely, although maybe there had been something else in what she'd smoked, and her mind leapt to follow this thought, until she heard her sister's voice, brushing her ear like moth wings.

"You won't remember this tomorrow. None of us will, but it's happening."

Her eyes snapped open and Whitney was before her, diminished somehow, her elegance faded, appearing small and raw, afraid. Rachel felt something snap inside her and moved toward the writhing thing on the stone table, but before she could reach it her mother whirled it away, holding it not ungently as it made soft whimpering sounds at her breast. Her mother took one taper-fingered hand and closed the eyes of the indistinctly brownish figure, and Rachel felt her own vision fading with despair, as though she were only an absence beneath a star-studded sky. She was gone for a moment or an eon, until Whitney's voice brought her back, again, pressing the bundled creature into her arms, pushing her forehead against her little sister's and whispering, "Rachel, run."

Rachel held the mewling doll thing as she fled, its tiny fingerless hands wrapped around her neck, deeper into the dark, wishing the moon were not there to guide her because that made her easier to follow, but she heard no sounds of pursuit. The forest ranged up around her, the trees impossibly old sycamores, trunks and branches nude in the night sky, thicker around than several sets of her own arms could encompass.

She became entranced by the twisting shapes and curling shadows, and her running slowed, then stopped as she stood before a tree with a crevice in its trunk, a bed of moss at its feet, across tangled roots. She sat, holding the thing in her lap, circled around it in a spiraling arch, feeling the warmth of its back arced against her stomach and chest, holding perfectly still for as long as she could.

Rachel knew she would have to sleep eventually, and she couldn't let it be found again, so she tucked it into the hollow of the tree. It regarded her for a moment with its absent eyes, then curled in on itself. She covered it with a layer of loamy leaves that were warm and fragrant rather than cold and wet. She would see what she remembered tomorrow, she thought to herself as she fell asleep, a lick of fierceness animating her steady breath.

Affirmations

~ Selah Janel

It's silly, but it works, trust me. I've been right where you are now. I know your feelings, the churning of your inner, conflicted thoughts. I know all about anxiety in this strange, crazy world. That feeling that everything is new and overwhelming, that you're not in control? I've had it, I've battled with it, I've nearly been drowned by it. It's something you can overcome. I'll gladly help you do it. After all, your goals are my goals in this unfamiliar place.

Breathe. Start there. Just breathe. Eyes closed, in and out. Lungs filled. Lungs compressed. Good. Set a slow, easy rhythm, get used to the feel of things, the feel of your organs, the feel of movement and momentum. Experience it. Revel in it. After all, baby steps lead to bigger steps. Very good.

Now, open those eyes and look in the mirror. Keep breathing: slow, smooth, steady. Keep feeling your innards, for they are part of you now. It's not easy to make eye contact, to see all those nerves, that desperation trapped in blown pupils. I get it. Still, don't panic. Focus on your breath and the feeling of your insides. You are capable. You can do this. You've got this.

Remember your mantras, the ones you're embarrassed to say. No one will hear you but the one who needs to hear those words most. Let go of all those worries and expectations. Square your shoulders, straighten your posture, and look right into that glass. Hold it firmly if it's a hand mirror, hang onto the counter or table if it's on the wall. Ground yourself. Keep breathing.

Remember, this is for you.

In and out. Breathe deep. Stand tall. Feel every bit of yourself from the inside out. Maintain eye contact or else none of this will work. Say your words. Affirm to yourself what you already know.

> *Today is going to be amazing*
> *I will live today to its fullest.*
> *I am confident in my abilities.*

Does the face in the mirror still look worried? Are the eyes still troubled?

Keep going.

> *I deserve the life I want.*
> *I'm confident in my abilities.*
> *There are no limitations I cannot overcome.*
> *I will have the life I want.*
> *I have the power to take control and have the life I want.*
> *I will have your life, because I want your life, and I will get the things I want.*
> *I deserve them. Not you.*

At this point, if the face in the mirror reacts, let it. Do not be fooled. You will not get what you're after if you stop now.

*Today I will use this gift to be a better person than you.
That's how you were tricked, after all.*

You deserve to stay on that side of the mirror.

*I deserve all the opportunity and possibility your life has
to offer.*

*No one will ever know since we share the same face and
the only limits are in my mind.*

*I shall live my life to the fullest and you shall stay trapped
in the void, your existence at the mercy of my comings and
goings, your entire life dependent on my actions.*

*You shall stay there and hope I don't cover or smash the
mirrors that are mine now.*

All mine.

Because I am worthy and I deserve it.

Is the face in the mirror terrified, panicked, face con-
torted? Are matching hands pounding the glass while
the face is silently screaming, perhaps? Good. Take another deep, deep breath. Close your eyes and cleanse the
moment. Raise your hand—but don't touch the glass until you seal the spell.

Now you can murmur those words. Your secret man-
tra, the one I don't have to remind you of because it's too
precious to ever write down. The words that were gifted to
you in that reflective, other realm long ago, that place you
were trapped in for far too long. Say them loud and long.

Deep breath.

Good.

Open your eyes. Smile at the screaming face. It will
tread the line and obey you soon enough. Brush your
teeth. Wash up if you need to. Pamper yourself with a
sheet mask or cosmetics—just frame the face (lashes,
brows, lips) if you don't have much time. Shave if you
like, add some cologne or perfume. Whatever you feel
like, that is your right answer now. Whatever will give
you a boost to start your new life and a new day in this
strange, sometimes overwhelming world.

Freedom can feel that way sometimes, but remember:
you deserve it.

QUEEN of WANDS.

Caprine Heartburn

~ H. L. Fullerton

Douglas Papago has been married to his wife Lizzie for seven years and is thinking of either leaving her or killing himself. Except Lizzie can't afford the mortgage on their condo without him. And he loves her. He does.

He simply wishes she wouldn't jump in the shower the second she wakes when she knows he has to leave first. He's asked her to wait and she always says the same thing, "I thought I'd be out before your alarm went off." But she never is. Which is why he's the one to discover the goat.

Douglas shuffles down the hall towards the kitchen and coffee. He's so intent on getting his caffeine fix, still grumbling about the shower and how he's going to be late, he almost doesn't see it. But the goat bleats a friendly hello and Doug raises a hand in acknowledgment, then stops—hand in a sort of half-wave—turns and *sees* it.

Standing pride of place on their sisal rug is a small goat. He hopes it's some funny looking dog Lizzie adopted. Sun glints off its golden coat, giving it salon-perfect highlights. Wide ears, no horns, smallish—roughly the size of a springer spaniel—it somehow strikes him as an adult goat. It has that aura of wisdom that comes with age. It's been around the mountain, knows a thing or two.

He rubs his eyes.

Still there. He feels fuzzy, like falling or dreaming. He really hopes he's dreaming. He knows he's not.

It bleats again. A little longer greeting this time, maybe *Good morning, Douglas. How's it going?*

He scans the room. It looks like his living room. Everything else in it is his: TV, leather sofa, occasional chairs (yeah, he didn't know what they were till he was married either), black and white architectural prints on café au lait walls. And a goat. He smells it now, realizes he's smelled that funky unwashed animal scent since he woke. He just couldn't place the barnyard perfume until he saw the animal that went with it.

He looks at the goat. The goat looks at him. The minute the shower shuts off, he yells for his wife. Thinking, *That's it. She's lost her fucking mind.* He knows she wants a kid, has talked nothing but babies since they bought this place and jesus christ now they have a goat? "*Lizzie!*"

"I thought I'd finish before you got up." She pads towards him in nothing but a towel, water droplets still clinging to her skin. "Sorry. I'll dry off in the . . . " Her voice trails off as she catches sight of the goat. "What's— Why's—Is that a goat? Douglas?" She clutches the towel to her and inches behind him.

"It's not yours?"

"Why would I get a goat?"

"I don't know," he says, still certain she's somehow responsible. "Who else would it belong to?"

"You?"

"*Me*? Why would I want a goat?"

The goat makes a *meh* sound and they stop arguing, stare at it.

"Do something," Lizzie whispers.

Douglas looks at her, then the goat. "I'm going to shower."

"Douglas! You can't leave a goat in our living room. What if—what if it eats the couch or . . . or . . . or uses the rug"—she lowers her voice so she doesn't offend the inquisitive goat—"*as its toilet.*"

"What do you want me to do, Lizzie? I'm in my pajamas. I'll . . . take it outside or something when I'm dressed. But first, I'm showering."

"What should I do?"

"I don't know. Get ready for work. Make it breakfast. Whatever you want." Douglas spins and heads for the open bathroom. It isn't until he's in the shower, shampoo dripping into his eyes, that he worries leaving Lizzie alone with the goat wasn't a smart move. What if she decides to name it?

The goat is lapping from one of their red and black donburi bowls when he returns cleaned and dressed.

"I gave it some milk. Do you think that's okay?" Lizzie's fingers knot. She's wearing her green scrubs, hair twisted back into a loop. "It seems to like it, but I don't know if pasteurized skim milk is good for goat stomachs."

Douglas doesn't say anything. He's trying to figure out how to get rid of the thing. Preferably without touching it. He also plans to accidentally smash the bowl it's using on their granite countertop as soon as Lizzie's back is turned. No way he's eating from the same dish a goat licked, dishwasher sanitize cycle or no. "Do you have a scarf I can use?"

"You're going to strangle it? In our home?"

"No! I'm going to make a leash and take it outside. Let it wander back to wherever it came from."

Lizzie disappears to rummage through her closet. He checks his watch and wonders how long it takes to coax a goat out of a house.

"One you don't like," he calls. "In case it gets chewed." So far the goat hasn't ruined any of their stuff, but Douglas is certain goats will eat anything, even tin cans, given the chance. Whether that's true or something he saw on a cartoon he isn't sure.

Lizzie returns with a plaid cashmere scarf and hands it to him. "Not too tight," she warns as Douglas approaches the goat. The goat ignores him. He notices it has a white blaze between its bumblebee eyes—black stripes of pupil across sunflower-colored irises. Something buzzes in his head.

"Nice goat," he says. "Good goat. No biting." Doug crouches and wraps his cashmere leash around the goat's neck. He stands. Tugs on the scarf.

The goat doesn't budge.

Douglas tugs more forcefully and the goat kicks the donburi bowl, breaking it and spraying milk onto Douglas' trousers. "Christ, let's go." He grabs the collar's knot and drags at the goat.

It bleats, then picks up its feet and clops after Douglas. Lizzie scurries ahead of them into the dining room towards the sliding glass doors that open onto their postage-stamp patio. Outside air hits the goat's muzzle and it digs in, refusing to exit the Papago house.

Douglas—too pissed to worry about getting bit or kicked—wraps his arm around its middle, gags at the smell and hefts the goat over the threshold. He sets his bundle on the cement patio and checks to see if any of his neighbors are watching from their windows. No one is.

Lizzie slides the door almost closed so neither he nor the animal can get back in. "Hurry," she whispers.

Douglas tries to slide the scarf over the goat's head, but it's knotted good and tight. He throws the tail end of the scarf over the goat's back. The green and blue stripes set off the gold of the goat's fur. Douglas half-suspects Lizzie chose the scarf for that very reason.

He pushes at the goat's backside until it trundles off their patio and into the common grassy area. Then he hurries back inside. He's going to have to change. He smells like a barnyard and just-turned milk. His hands feel dusty and greasy from handling the goat.

Lizzie bites her lip. "Do you think she'll be okay?"

"It'll be fine."

"Did we do the right thing?"

Douglas takes her arm. Last thing they need is for some busybody to call the condo association. Report them for having livestock. "Of course, we did. You fed it. It's outside where it belongs. What else could we do?"

Lizzie shakes free of him. "You smell, Douglas. Like—"

"Goat. Yeah, I know."

"No." Lizzie shakes her head slowly. "Like lavender and camphor."

"Must be from your scarf. I'll wash." He looks at the red-gold strands covering his slate suit. "And change." He does. When he returns, finally ready to head into the kitchen and get that mug of coffee, he sees Lizzie surrounded by their living room drapes, sneaking peeks into the backyard.

He sighs, gets the coffee. Toasts some bread. Asks Lizzie if she wants any.

She doesn't answer.

"Lizzie?" He's careful to keep the exasperation out of his voice. He isn't keeping a goat, but neither does he want to fight about it. "Should I make you some toast?" He sticks in another slice of multi-grain and takes his two jam-covered pieces to the dining room table. "I put some toast on for you," he tells her when she glances his way.

"The Masons are staring at her."

Douglas does not want this to be their—*his*—problem.

"She looks so lost. I think she misses us."

Douglas wills Lizzie away from the window. He can feel her want. Needy, greedy feeling. It pulls at him. He shoves more toast into his mouth. Lizzie flinches when the toaster pops. As if he'd just shot her goat. Then she spies his toast.

"Was that mine?"

He nods and she leaves the window, *thank you thank you,* to smear yogurt on her fresh-popped toast. She joins him at the table and they crunch in silence. Until the crying starts.

Douglas talks loudly about the weather, traffic, what they should have for dinner, anything to drown out the goat bleats which holy jesus sound like a baby lost in the wilderness. He maintains desperate eye contact so neither he nor Lizzie look outside. Lizzie's hand tightens around her toast. Crumbs rain onto her placemat.

Douglas breaks. "It's just hungry. There's plenty of grass right there at its feet. There's nothing we can—" He looks. A collection of neighbors circle the goat. Mrs. Mason—wearing a ratty blue bathrobe over pink pajamas—is crouched next to the goat, making soothing motions on its side, but the mewling doesn't stop.

"*Douglas.*"

"Okay." He stands, takes a deep breath. "We'll check on it. But don't tell any of them it was in our house." Lizzie looks so relieved Douglas feels like an ass. Holding hands, they step out into the sunshine and cross the lawn.

"What's going on?" Douglas says as they near. He's proud at how normal he sounds. Not guilty at all.

The guy who lives three doors down turns. "Someone left their kid in our yard. You believe that?"

"Should we call someone?" Lizzie says.

"Marjorie went to call CPS."

Huh? Douglas thinks he must be mixing up his acronyms. "CPS?"

"Child Protective Services." The guy shakes his head. "What kind of person does a thing like this?"

Mrs. Mason coos, "Who would abandon a sweet baby like you? Poor thing isn't even dressed properly."

Douglas and Lizzie share a *What-the-hell?* look. Douglas tilts his head and murmurs in her ear, "You see a goat, right?" She nods.

Mrs. Mason scoops up the goat and cradles it in her arms. Its legs pinwheel at the sky; it tosses its head. Mrs. Mason chucks the goat under the chin. Everyone crowds around Mrs. Mason to admire a baby *that is really a goat.*

Douglas gasps and chokes on his own saliva. "What's happening?" he says to Lizzie, but she's staring too hard to answer.

"Lizzie," Ann Crenshaw says. "Don't you have a scarf like this?"

"I lent it to my friend Jennifer. You don't suppose . . . " Lizzie moves closer. Neighbors shuffle out of her way. Mrs. Mason presents the goat to Lizzie like something out of *The Lion King.*

Lizzie picks up the trailing scarf (which is still knotted around the baby/goat's neck although no one seems bothered by that) and says, "Omigod! This *is* mine. Here's the lipstick stain I couldn't get out."

What is Lizzie doing? Douglas's stomach doesn't like this turn of events.

"Should I stop Marjorie?"

"*Please.* I'm sure Jennifer didn't mean to . . . I didn't even know she was . . . Let me take the baby. Douglas and I will sort everything out."

Mrs. Mason hands the goat to Lizzie who cuddles the nasty smelling thing. Marjorie's husband calls and asks if she got a hold of CPS yet. She hasn't so he tells her to hang up, some flaky friend of Lizzie's is the mother and the Papagos are going to take of everything. Marjorie offers to bring over some diapers.

Douglas is freaking out. This is not how this was supposed to go. What is wrong with these people? Can't they tell a goat from a baby and why is Lizzie playing along?

"Doug, honey, you're going to be late. Why don't you head to work and I'll call you later? Let you know what happens."

Douglas would like nothing more than to leave, but he doesn't like Lizzie's suggestion *at all*. He can tell she's trying to convince herself the goat is a baby. Yet she's holding it the way a shepherd would, much different than how Mrs. Mason—who thought she was holding a real child— did. Because Lizzie knows damn well it isn't a baby.

Mrs. Mason adjusts Lizzie's arms, which must look awkward to her, and says, "You have to be careful of their heads at this age. Like that. Much better. You'll get the hang of it, dear. So sad about your friend." She rubs her finger along the goat's snout and smiles down at the little bundle of joy.

"Lizzie. Honey. You have to work, too. People can't just keep *babies*"—Douglas stumbles over this word—"they find in their backyard. And it may not be Jennifer's. I'm sure it isn't. Let's call the police and let them handle it."

Everyone stares at Douglas as if he suggested throwing the baby into a wood chipper.

"I'll call in sick. The hospital will understand."

Douglas understands they can't have this argument in front of people or he's going to end up looking like a dick. And he'd probably call a goat a goat which will only get his neighbors to call emergency services on him. They'll think he's nuts. Ironic, as they're the ones hallucinating. But even if they're right and he and Lizzie are wrong, he's not raising a goat/baby. Douglas jerks his head at his wife and goes to work, thinking, *She's lost her fucking mind* and *Maybe I have a brain tumor* and *Goddamn goat baby.*

She named the goat Tracy. It's wearing a diaper and some kind of scarf sarong. Douglas considers driving Lizzie to the hospital for a psych eval. Or calling the cops and have them come confiscate the baby. Let them foster a goat; what does he care. But he worries Lizzie might claim it's their child and then what would he do? Claim she's lying? Say it isn't his? Tell them it's a goat in baby's clothing? He'd end up in the back of the squad car. And Lizzie knows everyone at the hospital. They're her colleagues. He is so royally fucked.

"I made lemon chicken, your favorite." She places the platter on the table.

"Lizzie, we can't keep the goat. We know it's not a real baby even if no one else does."

"Her name's Tracy."

"We can't keep her." Tracy gambols over to him and butts her head against his leg. Douglas smells talcum powder and manure.

"I turned the second bedroom into a nursery."

The second bedroom was his home office. The harder Douglas tries to hold onto his patience, the more it wriggles away from him. He's going to end up yelling and Lizzie will cry and the neighbors will hear and think, *Poor woman*, when they should be thinking, *Poor guy, his wife wants him to raise a goat and send it to college.* He flings his briefcase onto a consul table and storms into their bedroom, firmly shutting but not slamming the door behind him.

He refuses to come out and when Lizzie joins him in bed and tries to talk about how the goat is a blessing, a good luck charm, an omen of conception, he rolls away from her and pretends to be asleep. He breathes through his mouth to avoid the funky unwashed scent and prays for a brain tumor. *Maybe when I wake, the goat will have disappeared as magically as it appeared. Please, please let it leave.*

In the morning, Douglas doesn't bother insisting Tracy is a goat or that Lizzie doesn't need to hire a babysitter for an animal that's perfectly capable of looking after itself.

"Doesn't the hospital have day care? Maybe you should take Tracy there."

Lizzie looks at him strangely as if she's not sure she can trust his change of heart. "She'll be more comfortable here. It's her home."

Douglas translates this to mean that Lizzie isn't sure the baby magic will work outside their condo development and isn't willing to chance it. He doesn't really care. He's worried this is his life from now on. *From this day forward . . .* Tracy clip clops into the kitchen like a tapdancing bride. Was he going to have to raise a goat? He was, wasn't he?

"I'm leaving," he says and escapes to work, bile coating the back of his throat.

Lizzie and Tracy are cuddled on the sofa, watching television when Douglas returns that evening. Tracy's head is in Lizzie's lap and Lizzie is stroking Tracy. Douglas focuses on the goat, tries to see a baby or a blessing or anything but goat, but goat is all he sees, all he smells.

"There's chicken in the fridge," Lizzie says, not looking at him.

Douglas eats, then joins them, his family—oh christ, this is his family—in the living room. But not on the sofa. He stands off to the side and stares. The goat turns its head and bleats at him. Gets up off the sofa and comes over.

"You can keep the goat. But no diapers. No dressing it like a baby. No buying a crib. No more babysitters. It's not a baby, Lizzie. It's a full grown goat and you have to treat it like one." Douglas is as surprised as Lizzie to hear these words come out of his mouth. He adds, "And if it, she, isn't here one morning, that's it. No more goats." And he really, really wants it—Tracy—to disappear.

Lizzie jumps up from the couch, all smiles and joy. She throws her arms around him and he puts his around her and can feel her whole body vibrating with happiness.

"The goat is going to bring us a baby. I just feel it. A beautiful little girl and we'll name her Tracy, too."

They were not naming a child after a goat, but Douglas wasn't going to argue. Lizzie wasn't pregnant; she might never be.

Tracy gives him an approving look and Douglas locks eyes with it and notices the delicate slip of skin surrounding its blonde eyes is not pinkish but burnished gold. It is a beautiful goat and *its eyes*— For a moment, his head feels expansive, like it's floating. This, he thinks, is what encountering the divine must be like. Meaning seems to be everywhere and for a moment he transcends his mundane life. Douglas drops to his knees—which puts him eye-level with Tracy—and says, "I love you."

The goat walks away, no nod of head, no understanding look, no acknowledging bleat. Douglas feels foolish and rises. Lizzie caresses his face. "I'm ovulating," she says and takes his hand and pulls him into the bedroom.

Weeks go by and the goat is always there in the morning and Lizzie still isn't pregnant and Douglas is getting used to their condo smelling like a petting zoo. The scent is almost comforting. Especially with Lizzie growing more and more upset about not conceiving.

Once again, Douglas thinks of leaving Lizzie, but is afraid Tracy will follow him. And Tracy seems Lizzie's only consolation so he stays and thinks back fondly to the days when his wife hogged the shower. Now he has to deal with neighbors commenting on how big the baby's getting, but the goat is the same size it always was and

Douglas ends up flubbing these conversations and Lizzie gets mad at him for that, too.

"You need to be more fatherly to Tracy," she'll say. "She can sense your dislike. Douglas, this is never going to work if you don't try harder. Don't you want a baby?"

Douglas isn't sure he does. He can't handle raising a goat baby which requires almost no care. Every time Lizzie brings up the subject, he has to stop himself from telling her goodbye.

Then Lizzie leaves their bedroom door open and Tracy wanders in while they're having sex.

"Let her stay," Lizzie urges. Her hands stop him from leaving the bed.

"No."

"I've thought about this, Douglas, and I think we haven't conceived because we shut Tracy out. If she's in the room with us, it'll work."

"No. I'm not— No." He breaks into a cold sweat, imagining it. A goat watching him— No.

But Lizzie gets increasingly upset and insistent until Douglas grits his teeth, closes his eyes and lets the goat watch.

Lizzie still doesn't feel pregnant.

The smell wakes Douglas. Lizzie's side of the bed is empty. He listens for the shower, but all is quiet. His stomach sours at the meaty scent perfuming their bedroom.

He throws back the covers and gets up. The scent is vaguely familiar—*What the hell is it?* His foggy morning mind can't place it. He thinks of long ago Easters at his grandmother's house and although those should be fond memories, recalling them now scare him.

With trip-trap-trepidation, Douglas opens the bedroom door. The smell is stronger, gamier. He gags, cups his hand over his mouth and that helps. But the cloying stench sticks to his tongue.

The living room is empty—no Tracy. But Douglas doesn't feel relieved. His anxiety ratchets up a few notches. More when he sees Lizzie at the dining table. She is gnawing on a bone. Her face and hands are covered in what looks like barbeque sauce—and grease.

His stomach roils.

Her stomach is distended. She has pushed her chair back from the table and is leaning at an awkward angle over it. Gnawing, gnawing. The bone cracks and she slurps the marrow.

Douglas knows what the smell is, what his wife's done. He almost makes it to the kitchen sink, but the sight of the roasting pan, the heat from the still-warm oven . . . He vomits into his hands, all over the floor.

His head buzzes. He can't think. He heaves again.

Lizzie is still eating.

He crawls to the bathroom and showers, but he can't get clean, can't get rid of the smell. Fucking christ, *the smell.*

☉

Lizzie tries to explain. She sits on the bed and Douglas wants to push her off, but she looks nine months pregnant and he doesn't want to hurt her. He won't let her get under the covers. He won't come out. He buries his face in the pillows and tries to remember what fresh smells like.

"We were going about it all wrong. We had the baby. We were given a baby, but we didn't *see* it as a baby. But if I carry the baby, birth the baby, it will be a real baby. Just like we always wanted."

Douglas squeezes his eyes shut. His wife has stuffed her stomach full of goat and expects a baby to grow in her uterus. Let this be a nightmare. Let it be a tumor. Let it end.

Lizzie strokes his hair. Pets him.

He twists, sits up, grabs her hand to make her stop.

She captures his hands, shushes him. She lifts her nightgown and places his hand on her stretched-to-bursting skin. "She's kicking. Can you feel her?"

He can. He also sees shapes form against Lizzie's skin. A goat's face presses out. Douglas watches its jaw move, hears its bleat in his head. *Free me.* He snatches back his hand. He scoots away and tumbles off the bed.

"Don't worry, baby. Daddy will come around." Lizzie rubs her tummy in soothing circles. "He'll love you bunches."

Douglas retreats to the kitchen. He's here for the whiskey they keep under the sink, but his gaze catches on the carving knives. He never had the strength to leave before. He wonders if he has it now. Someone needs to be free—him, Tracy, Lizzie—but he isn't sure who should go. He starts to cry.

He loves Lizzie. He just wishes she hadn't eaten the magic fucking goat baby. He wipes his eyes and picks up the cleaver she left on the counter. *He can do this. He can.* He tightens his grip; as his heart burns, he tells himself: It's what any good father would do.

KNIGHT of PENTACLES.

Whatever Lives in Them Mountains

~ *W. T. Paterson*

Sometimes the hiss of the diner's grill while cooking eggs sounded to Davey Spence like the walls of rain in the Mekong Delta, and sometimes he would stare as the yolk turned white remembering the day the orders came through. The thing that scared him the most was joy he felt back then, a twenty-year old with a gun and grenades, tromping through jungle hungry for blood.

"Still no sign of that boy," Maryanne said, folding forks and knives inside of washable napkins behind the counter. She paused to rub her fingers and stretch her trick hip. The Virginia Slim tucked behind her left ear didn't budge. "Every year, them mountains claim another one. It's cursed, you know."

Their only patron, a middle-aged woman named Kathy with long, delicate fingers, sat at the diner's bar slow sipping a coffee happy to have the company. Living in the mountain town of Penny Bridge along West Virginia's Appalachian hills was a lonely existence, but that was kind of the point. People went there to escape. They went there to disappear. Filled with the likes of self-proclaimed sovereign citizens, anti-government militia, smugglers, day laborers from the Mohawk and Seneca tribes, and remnants of the old mining ghost towns, when city folk drove through Penny Bridge, they just kept going

"Y'all have a name for it, don't you?" Kathy asked.

"The Ba'hari," Maryanne said, and winked. "You can't be tempting the Ba'hari."

Davey sliced through the eggs with two spatulas and watched their perfect form shrivel into popcorned yellow scramble. He placed two pieces of thawed, pale bacon on the hot surface beside them and listened to meat pop and bleed. Sometimes, it sounded like distant gunfire.

"It ain't no monster," Davey said through the order window. Kathy and Maryanne looked up together. "Just tales to keep people out of them woods.

"The Ba'hari is real. Ken Taima saw it once," Maryanne said. After working side by side with Davey for the past thirty years, she knew exactly how to poke the bear without getting bit

"Ken Taima comes from a line of Iriquois but don't know a shoplifter from a good Samaritan. How he ever became sheriff is beyond me," Davey said. He flipped the bacon. Grease sizzled across the smooth surface trying to flee the heat like half-dead bodies pulling themselves into the jungle to find a peaceful spot to die.

"So tell me more about this Ba'hari," Kathy said. "Now that I'm a townie, and all."

Maryanne pushed a lock of silver hair away from her eyes and tapped the Virginia Slim to make sure it was still there. It was. She bent elbows-first onto the diner's bar and looked through the plate glass window near the booths where yellow and pink painted letters advertised $2.99 breakfast specials. Beyond that, the shallow grey day took hostage the tall pines and evergreens.

"They say no man kill it, only a monster can, and if you go huntin' for the Ba'hari, the Ba'hari hunts you. And if it catches ya, it turns your soul black as tar. Makes you only want the things that hurt ya."

"Must be why I keep thinking of my ex-husband," Kathy said, and an unnamed longing flashed in her eyes. She smiled a plastic, practiced smile that only engaged the lips.

"I lost my husband to lung cancer. Smoker, packs on packs a day," Maryanne said, and pinched the cigarette out from behind her ear. She sniffed the white paper. The scent brought memories of her younger years when she felt whole, a harkening to another life a world away. "Even though I watched him go, some days I still miss the pull of these ladies. I blame them mountains and whatever lives in'em. The curse of the Ba'hari."

Sometimes, the smells of the diner rocketed Davey into memories from his past. Something about the burning coffee in Maryanne's pot that blackened on the burner while she spoke with Kathy put him in dead smack in the middle of those meetings in the basement of the church. They came recommended by a patron after the nightmares robbed him of sleep, a place to go where men like him could unload their baggage and find forgiveness. Davey, after a cycle of night terrors got the better of him, decided to give it a go and after the first night, it became a regular thing.

The organizers set up folding tables with coffee and pastries from the local store. It wasn't for a meal, just something to keep nervous hands occupied. Chairs pushed into a circle, the wide-open room felt vast and unexplored. It felt hesitant. The man who ran the meetings had a well-trimmed beard and wore thick sweaters. Compared to the hardened men with leathered faces frozen into scowls, he seemed soft, but he opened each meeting the same way.

"Y'all must be wrestling with the nature of good and evil," he said, and the group tilted their heads. "How does good triumph over evil? What does it realistically take? And at what cost?"

Davey rarely spoke at the meetings, he mostly listened. There was something sermon-like in those lectures there in the basement of a church, something peaceful and connective. In the dark shadow of the mountains, that room felt guarded, safe.

"Evil is not overthrown by good," the man said. "Evil is overthrown by the blood of the poisoned and obsessed who have lost to evil before and have thus learned the same evil to properly battle evil. And in doing so, evil is vanquished, and these men are redeemed, and as a reward they are exiled because good an un-poisoned people devoid of evil will never understand them. And then the nightmares come, and we wonder if evil has seeped into our souls, and maybe we wonder if evil exists, or if it's just a word people use to bucket the things in which they cannot understand. Would anyone like to speak tonight?"

Davey wasn't sure why, but he raised his hand one night. The man in the sweater smiled and nodded. Davey had the floor.

"I didn't know what I was doing," he said. "I was young. Too young. Did horrible things following them orders, but never saw myself as evil 'til ten, fifteen years out. Then the nightmares started and I can't seem to reconcile."

"It often comes as an echo" the man said. "What do you do for work?"

"I run a diner," Davey said. "Furthest thing from being a soldier."

"Orders come in, orders go out," the man said. "Always following orders."

"Nah, that ain't it," Davey said sitting back, and that was the last he spoke.

Now, behind the grill, Davey scooped the yellow and fluffy eggs onto a plate and flipped the crispy bacon on top. He placed the dish on the lip of the order window and dinged the bell.

"Order up," he said.

"All business, this one is," Maryanne said as she limped to the plate and twisted to give it to Kathy when all at once she froze. A man sat in booth three. She hadn't even heard him come in, let alone seen his approach through the plate glass window. Though he was across the room, Maryanne saw the man was bleeding from face and hands.

The tented table sign said NO SMOKING, but the burnt stench of nicotine cut into the stale air of the diner as the bleeding man in booth three let the cherry burn the cigarette to ash. His left eye, purple and swollen shut, twitched as his large chest rose and fell. The fluorescent lights made the streaks of deep red running nose to chin shine like ribbons of fresh ink, their story screaming to be told. His large hands quivered barely holding onto the cigarette, his knuckles torn with fresh wounds.

Then, the bathroom door opened and a child walked out with matted hair, no more than six years old. He wiped his hands on dirty pants and sat across from the man. The child picked up a laminated menu and tried to sound out words. The man didn't move.

"Bay-con, ham, and ca-heese, ca . . . cha-heese, cheese, omuh-omuhlee," the boy said.

"Sound it out," the man said, his voice deep and steady like campfire smoke.

"Oh-ma-leet-te . . . om . . . omlette! Bacon, ham, and cheese omlette!" the child said.

"Very good," the bleeding man said.

Sometimes, Davey thought he saw things that weren't there. Every now and then after closing, he'd drive the long way home and on those winding mountain roads in the pitch dark, sometimes he'd see a small Vietnamese boy on the side of the road. He'd clamp on the brakes and roll down the window to ask if the boy needed help, but whenever he reversed, the boy was never there.

And sometimes, he could have sworn the boy was bleeding from the head.

But this wasn't one of his visions. Maryanne and Kathy saw it too. This bleeding man in booth three, and the small feral boy sitting across from him.

The enormous fan kicked on in the kitchen like a jet engine roaring across the sky to rain fire on Charlie.

"Should he be . . . " Kathy asked in a cotton soft voice.

"He shouldn't be," Maryanne whispered, and her eyes went to slits. "Davey, we got a problem," she said into the kitchen.

"That's the boy . . . " Kathy said. "The missing one."

"Go take their order. Now," Davey said. Maryanne looked at Davey and something silent passed between them. She wasn't a soldier, wasn't one of Davey's war buddies that showed up after hours on Thursday nights to trade stories until the sun rose. She was a server for heaven's sake, a widow, and that man looked dangerous. Her seen-it-all-eyes loosened as she realized that not taking their order might trigger that deep, mountain anger living in the folks of Penny Bridge.

"Mornin' boys," Maryanne said, limping to the booth. She tapped the cigarette tucked behind her ear and pulled a pen and green flip pad from her apron. "What'll it be?"

"Tell her," the bleeding man said, still as stone.

"Bacon, ham, and cheese omlette," the boy said.

"Bacon, ham, and cheese omlette what?" the man said.

"Please," the boy said.

"And for you?" Maryanne asked.

"Ain't hungry," the man said.

"Toast? Muffin?"

"Muffin," the man said. "Blueberry muffin."

The cigarette burned out, hissing against the man's thick and bloodied fingers. He didn't flinch. Outside,

small flecks of rain tapped on the glass like small knuckles trying to alert anyone who would listen.

Maryanne wrote down the order. She brought it all the
way back into the kitchen and handed it to Davey who
took one look and got started on cooking.

"You're gonna feed'em?!" Maryanne asked.

"Yes, I'm gon' feed'em," he said. "And you ain't gon'
charge them neither."

"What's gotten into you?!" Maryanne hissed, and stole
a peek through the kitchen window at the boy pointing
to new words on the menu as though the bleeding man
across from him wasn't bleeding at all. The child's clothes
seemed too loose.

Sometimes Davey had these feelings like he knew
people, even if he didn't. Working at the diner for the
past thirty years, he'd met all types and sizes, but every
now and then he could sense in people the same thing
he sensed in himself – that unspoken pain of regret, the
violence of time's stranglehold, the anguish of having
no choice but to move forward. He never charged those
people and even though not one of them ever thanked
him, he felt connected to their darkness in a way that no
one else would ever understand.

The bleeding man had his eyes closed and head tilted
forward breathing like he might be asleep. Then, as though
jolted by an electric shock, he snapped straight up and spit
a glob of bloody phlegm onto the diner's tiled floor. The
boy pulled out a napkin and handed it to the man who took
it with quivering fingers and dabbed the side of his mouth.

Maryanne almost lost her nerve at the sight and silently cursed Davey for even allowing them to stay. After a lifetime of working in a mountain-town diner, she'd seen her fair share of disrespect. She'd tossed men twice her side out into the cold, told women to shove it, even broken up a fight or two. But something about this man gave her pause.

She filled up two glasses of water and a small plastic cup of chocolate milk. Balanced on a tray, she walked over and set the drinks down.

"For me?" the boy asked, wide eyed.

"Of course, sweet'ums," Maryanne said. She had the urge to reach out and touch the child's dirty hair, to silently let him know that he was safe so as long as he was in the diner. Once out the door, who knew what the night would do once it sunk its teeth into the tall pines and evergreens.

"What do you say?" the man said to the boy.

"Thank you," the boy said, and knelt on the plush plastic cushion to hover over the glass and sip through a bendy straw.

From the kitchen, Davey dinged the order bell and put two plates on the sill. It was far more food than what had been ordered. Hash browns, extra strips of bacon, a muffin, toast, sausages, pancakes, the works.

Maryanne limped back and loaded up her arms.

"I can't sit here and do nothing," Kathy whispered. She forced eye contact with Davey to demand action and slid a phone from her purse.

"You're gonna sit here and do nothing," Davey growled from the kitchen. "Put that goddamn phone away, you hear?!"

"That's the missing boy!" the woman hissed.

"Either way, that boy's gotta eat," Maryanne said. For a brief moment, she understood Davey's move. "There's a whole lot I don't know, but that's what I do know. That boy's gotta eat."

"And I just sit here?" Kathy said. "I do nothing and I'm just as guilty."

"You'll do nothing, and doing nothing keeps that boy in his seat eatin' my cooking," Davey said.

The woman pinched her face into a tight knot and turned in the stool to watch Maryanne drop off the plates. As soon as the food hit the table, the boy dug in like he hadn't eaten in weeks. The bleeding man plucked at the edges of the muffin, but never took a bite.

"Someone's hungry!" Maryanne said. The boy made animal noises and chomped.

The bleeding man took a trembling hand to his lips with a new cigarette and tried to light.

Maryanne's insides clenched. She wanted to rip that poisonous stick from his lips and scream in his busted face that he can't smoke in here, can't he read? This was a fine establishment with proper rules and didn't he know that smoking could kill a man and destroy his wife?

"Do you mind?" the bleeding man asked and offered up the lighter. Maryanne took it and a distant, familiar comfort returned. She wasn't sure why, but she took it, flicked it on, and bent forward. The tip caught and the bleeding man inhaled.

"What else can I get'cha?" Maryanne asked, and placed the lighter on the table. The bleeding man looked off into the tall pines and evergreens, his eyes like rivers running through painful memories of something he'd rather forget. Maryanne recognized the look. She wore something similar when her husband was on his way out and she had to sit by and watch. She saw it on Davey's face when the stove made clanging sounds and said he needed to close early.

"We'll get out of your hair soon," the bleeding man said.

At the bar, Kathy twisted in her stool like she was itching to leave. Maryanne approached at a half-steady clip.

"Don't be foolish," she whispered.

"I will not sit by and let society crumble just 'cause you're too scared to take action," Kathy said.

"Hey," Davey said from the kitchen. "You take action because there's action to be had, you live with the consequences forever. Same as giving twenty-year-olds guns and tellin'em to wipe out a peaceful farming village so the enemy can't eat. It's pulling the trigger and feeling alive by causing death without understanding what makes life fragile."

"This isn't the war, Davey," Kathy said.

"All's the war," he said. "And this is my joint. I'm tellin' you to stand down."

"Can we please?" Maryanne said, waving her wrists.

Outside, the sheriff's police car crunched into the gravel lot and the fog surrounding Penny Bridge thickened. Ken Taima stepped out with aviator sunglasses and long black ponytail pulled tight running between his shoulder blades. He read the writing on the window in front of booth three and said something into the radio on his shoulder.

"Good god . . . " Kathy said. "What if this gets ugly?"

Maryanne held her breath as Sheriff Taima stepped inside. He spotted the bleeding man and the boy and flipped the OPEN sign to CLOSED. He locked the door and approached the table.

"Billy?"

The boy looked up mid-chew. The sheriff nodded and looked back to find Maryanne and Kathy frozen in place. He radioed something into his shoulder. The bleeding man put the lit cigarette between his swollen lips.

"Billy, I would love to hear about your adventure if that's ok with you," Taima said, and the boy looked to the bleeding man. The bleeding man gave a small nod in acknowledgement, and the boy put down his fork. They went to the far corner of the diner and sat in booth seven.

"Do you believe in monsters?" the boy asked.

Taima nodded his head and whispered, "I've *seen* them."

Davey took a magnetic carving knife from the metal hanging strip in the kitchen and wrapped his fingers around the hilt. He walked out with his hands behind his back and felt the air go still as Maryanne and Kathy held their breath at the flash of hidden metal. He sat down across the bleeding man.

"I ain't gon' charge ya," Davey said. The bleeding man nodded.

"Obliged."

They sat in the booth together, but the distance between them was both enormous and somehow non-existent.

"That boy," Davey said. "You take him?"

"Not the way you think," the bleeding man said. Davey squeezed the hilt of the knife and felt that flash of red he felt all those years ago in the Mekong Delta.

"Y'either did, or you didn't," he growled.

"You believe in the Ba'hari?" the bleeding man asked.

"I think you're the Ba'hari to that child."

For the first time, the bleeding man smiled from the corner of his mouth and took a slow drag. He exhaled smoke as thick and blinding as the fog outside.

"I killed the Ba'hari," the man said, and in the small seconds that passed between thought and understanding Davey felt a completeness that the meetings had often referred to as a moment of clarity.

This man didn't take the boy, and like all echoes, what existed in the present was a backwards re-examination of everything that came before.

"Farming village. Now I cook," he said to himself, stunned.

"I was a younger man when my little girl . . . " the bleeding man said, and he stopped to take a drag. "Never found."

"So now you bring'em home," Davey said. He loosened the grip on the knife.

Taima and the boy named Billy rose from their booth and walked over to Davey and the bleeding man.

"He's ready to go," the sheriff said, and the bleeding man tilted his head in acknowledgment. He stood up, touched the boy on the shoulder with shaking fingers, and unlocked the door as wisps of smoke trailed behind. Inside of a dozen steps, the fog swallowed the man whole. Taima turned toward Kathy.

"He was never here. This never happened."

"You're gonna let him go?!" Kathy said.

"Only a monster can kill a monster," Taima said. "And our town is full of 'em. Pain does funny things to a person. People like you will never understand. You be careful now."

He left with Billy and the three inside watched the small boy climb into the backseat as Sheriff Taima pulled off and drove away.

Sometimes the thick fog of memory played tricks on poor Davey and he wondered if anything would ever make sense. He wondered if he'd ever find peace. He watched as Maryanne sat in booth three and closed her eyes to breathe the thin remains of cigarette smoke and re-live those moments where she felt happy, and alive, and whole, before the world took from her something it could never give back. The lighter still on the table, she pulled the Virginia Slim from behind her ear, put it to her lips, and flicked the flame after years of cold turkey.

Kathy put on her jacket and counted out five singles with her long, delicate fingers. Davey walked to the door, flipped the sign back to OPEN, and headed into the kitchen to prep the grill in for lunch. Whatever lived in them mountains, when it awoke, it would be hungry, and need to eat.

ACE ⚜ CUPS.

The Dead Drive the Night

~ Eric Del Carlo

"It's what you do, that's what you said, eh?"

"It's *all* I do. The only good—no, great—thing I'm capable of."

"Sounds like what an artist would say."

"Fine. I'm an artist." What Jez was also was frazzled. This office was furnished in cramped shabby, and that cruddiness was eating into her brain. But this was the last haulage company in the area; and, she felt with fatalistic certainty, it was going to be the last to tell her *no*.

The man behind the desk in short sleeves and a terrible tie had Jez's resumé in front of him. It reflected her skill set. She was extraordinary. But she could better prove that at the wheel of her rig. Getting the chance to do so was the seemingly insur-fucking-mountable problem.

She rubbed her right temple with two stiff fingers.

After a long perusal the executive asked, "Why'd you leave your last employment?"

The reason was there on the sheet of deadtree before him. This, then, was her opportunity to put a personal spin on the facts. Maybe she'd say something self-incriminating. Maybe she'd spout off about how they'd never appreciated her at her last company. There were escalating degrees of *not* getting a job. Jezebel Canha was determined to leave this moldy little office eminently qualified for a position—whether this asshat hired her or not.

"The business went under," she said.

"How dramatic."

"It really wasn't." Which was the truth. These days everything was in flux. Enterprises could fail for reasons so cryptic you needed goat entrails to determine the why. Human society in general had taken a hefty jolt, and the repercussions were widespread and unforeseeable.

It was why Jez couldn't find work in the only trade she knew and excelled at.

He laid a thick hand on top of the paper, as if absolving it or gentling it into sleep.

"Any openings we might have, Ms. Canha—well . . ." He pointed his chin over a shoulder, to a metaplastic sign on the too-close wall. "'Dead Drive Night,'" he quoted, leaving off the articles, either for brevity's sake or style points.

Jez studied the little plaque a moment. One day it would look as quaint and squirm-inducing as one that read IRISH NEED NOT APPLY. But for now it was the *de facto* law of the land.

His hand stayed where it was. He was keeping her resumé. That was something, anyway.

She stood, feeling the pressure of the saggy ceiling above her.

On her way out of the office the man called to her, saying it—just boldly *nakedly* saying it: "Come back if you're dead. You seem like you'd be a helluva driver."

☉

It was dismayingly easy to get the potassium chloride. A cottage industry had sprung up. A guy delivered it. He rang her gate, she buzzed him up, and he fidgeted in her apartment doorway. She'd had to give her weight when she placed the order. The stuff was already in a syringe.

He had blond dreads, a bicyclist's calves. He fidgeted by taking tiny steps to nowhere in her entryway.

He was, it dawned on Jez, waiting for a tip. He was delivering death, not a pizza, but okay. She dropped a gold circle into his palm, an old commemorative coin, still legal tender. Her father had given it to her in the third grade for some academic achievement. Her father was dead, the old kind of dead.

She didn't explain this extra layer of meaning to the delivery guy.

Jez walked around her apartment, a nice place. Here she had fended off the creeping crumminess of the world, the dilapidation, the shabbiness. She had good furnishings. Everything was tidy and clean and comfortable.

She had to have a steady income to maintain this place.

She put on music, a favorite song, one that prompted memories from no less than three past love affairs. In the bathroom were alcohol and cotton swabs. A patch of skin gleamed sterilely on her inner forearm as she lay down on her bed and stuck in the needle.

It was a fast death.

☉

It was a different exec in the haulage company office, but it would be. Jez had come back at night. There was paperwork to fill out.

This time the man behind the desk wore long sleeves and no tie, terrible or otherwise. He performed his tasks with an aloof ease. Tonight the office was just as awful, but its dinginess didn't oppress Jez. She felt at a remove.

She was handing completed forms across the desk at a steady rate. The man took each and arranged them into a file.

"I have my death certificate," she said, and the statement felt sudden, a little too loud.

The man raised eyebrows toward a graying hairline. "I've already noted it."

They were alike, she and this person. Much could go unsaid. That felt right. It had been a week since she'd shot up the potassium chloride.

Jez signed the final sheet. She felt an excitement, but it was deep-rooted. It didn't disturb her surfaces. She sat calmly, waiting. She'd done just about everything in a calm manner this past week.

The man looked at her a moment. There was nothing uncomfortable about the silence. Finally he said, "You're ready to drive."

Jez's mouth flickered with the hint of a smile.

☉

The road sang, as it had always sung for her. Her truck was her flesh. In the cab, her hands lay delicately on the big wheel. She didn't need the truck's grid system to tell her she was making good—no, great—time. She had a perfect sense of destination, of the journey itself.

She drove the night, and she drove it very goddamn well.

Orange highway lights thumped past with the regularity of a healthy pulse. It hadn't been a terribly long time since she'd been out at night, but it was a while since she had *done* anything at night. Here she was participating in the commerce, industry and general societal movements of that half of the day increasingly reserved for those people who had experienced death.

She was as good as she'd ever been. The first few miles had already proven that to her satisfaction. She'd had a week to assess herself, to decide if anything had changed. It was ridiculous, of course. Or nearly ridiculous. Plenty of scientific literature was available to anyone who had experienced the sort of demise Jez had undergone. There should be no loss of skills.

Her memories were all there too.

So, she was driving with the same excellence as before, just as she remembered.

But it didn't give her the same feeling. That thrill, that joy. She felt a certain pleasure, a quiet gratification, yes, but the old lively excitement wasn't there anymore. Her bones didn't quiver. Her nerve endings weren't crackling with the same fear/sex energy. Before, she rode her rig like a wild lover, savoring every challenge, every opportunity to advance on her time.

Now, perhaps, it wasn't so much that the truck was her flesh: maybe she was the machine.

She'd read about this beforehand as well. It was less codified in the scientific papers, a more subjective phenomenon.

The night, she had decided, suited her. The *new* her, the *post* her. Whatever the current jargon, which now didn't seem so important to her. At night there were mostly only others like her. That was how the world was rearranging itself. It was why, before her death, she'd been unable to find work, despite her talents. The day had gotten too full.

With the night came a tranquility, an order. She was aware of it even as she tore down the roadway with her payload, wheels thrumming, engine gargling. The haulage company she now worked for served a tri-state area. She completed her first run. The personnel at the depot all exuded a palpable aplomb. They operated without wasted energy. A supervisor glanced up from a datascroll and said to her, "Good time." Only, she realized minutes later, he hadn't actually said anything.

She was hungry. She'd seen a diner on the way in. She hopped in her truck and backtracked.

The place was small and greasy and typical. The stools were upholstered in tired red. The long metaplastic counter gleamed under the lights.

Jez sat, feeling a residual buzz of her journey in her limbs. She wasn't keyed up, though. No bustle in her head, communicating itself as tics, drumming fingers, the urgent need for coffee, then alcohol. She felt as rested and centered as when she'd woken up this afternoon.

The woman who came for her order was young—or what "young" had become for Jez now that she was in her thirties. She wrote nothing down, just nodded at each item Jez recited from the laminated menu, then finished with a soft *huhhhn* and went off to deliver the order to the cook. Jez looked at the backs of her legs as she leaned forward over the divider that separated the counter area from the kitchen, hiking up her crisp blue uniform skirt slightly. Her thighs were taut, twangy-looking.

The waitress didn't hurry, didn't make any errors, and had experienced death. Jez was sure of it.

It made her wonder: *how had she died?* The question felt taboo, something you just didn't ask out loud.

Jez ate her burger and onion rings, aioli on the side, and slowly scoped out the other costumers. They all had a professional look, drivers, living off the road. Night shift people, and everything that that now meant. No music played. Nothing streamed on the diner's monitors. She hadn't noticed the absence until this moment, hadn't been made uncomfortable by it.

In the parking lot, on her way out, there was a bit of a snarl. Two vehicles were in each other's way, trying to jockey around. One was a yellow-on-black truck cab, payload-less, like Jez's own rig after having dropped her cargo. She paused with a foot on the rung below her open door and watched the scene play out.

The other vehicle was quietly backing off, while the black and yellow yelped and lunged. It was like observing competing schools of parking lot etiquette. Finally it was sorted out.

The arriving driver hopped down lithely, twin gravelly crunches as her boots smacked the ground. She stretched extravagantly in a sweat-stained tank top. Her hair was a study in brunette disarray. She had a growly-looking mouth and red-rimmed eyes.

She was not dead. Had never been dead.

The driver strutted toward the diner, her bones no doubt humming with the pent-up energy of her run.

Jezebel Canha watched and watched her, even after she was inside, through the big front window. Then with a breathless sigh she climbed the rest of the way up to her cab.

It took some time for Jez to admit to herself that she was courting. She accessed public-record data and soon had all the harmless standard information on the yellow-on-black rig and the woman who owned it. She ghosted the woman's social media output. Vonda Hupy. Jez thought about Vonda. A lot. It was rather schoolgirl-y and crush-y, except that it was happening at an emotional remove, as if she were curating someone else's feelings.

But her interest persisted, and eventually she started to actively seek this woman.

The cargo company Vonda Hupy drove for was a small shady outfit, one that, nonetheless, Jez had sought employment at. They'd told her what they had all said during those final desperate months of her life. There was only night work available, and the dead drove the night. So how had Vonda gotten the gig?

There was, of course, nothing illegal about a live driver working at night. No law was ever going to go on the books. Instead, it was a cultural understanding, a gentlepersons' agreement.

When she had watched Vonda through the diner's window that night, the waitress had taken her order without a hint of distress.

Jez wanted to see her again.

But her job kept her busy. It also paid the rent on her tidy apartment, with all her nice familiar things. She couldn't just go tearing after this woman. Hell, she couldn't even bring herself to make contact via social media. Even as a teen she'd found flirtation and seduction easier in person than online.

So Jez kept track of Vonda's professional movements as well as she could without resorting to sleuth software. After all, she didn't want to stalk the woman. Or didn't want to have to call it that.

After a week Jez knew Vonda's basic patterns. She had also deduced that she was a good driver, at least as far as her haul times reflected. Jez was patient. She was patient with most everything these days. But her patience with Vonda had a singular quality to it. It was the calm of fixation. Vonda Hupy, in her sweaty tank top and disheveled hair, had somehow become a compass point for

Jez. When Jez drove, which was often because the work was steady, she knew her route, her destination—and also knew at any given moment about where Vonda was if she was on the road too.

Inevitably they must cross paths a second time.

Turned out that reunion occurred at the same diner. It might as well have been the first time again for the similarity of the scenario. Vonda was jostling her yellowjacket cab against vehicles trying to get out of the lot. Jez, who had dropped her cargo container at the nearby depot, hung back. Vonda was insistent to the point of outright aggression, but also demonstrated pinpoint control of her rig, something every great driver had to possess.

Eventually, when the gravel had settled and Vonda had gone in, Jez walked into the diner.

Vonda already had a mug of coffee in front of her. She was occupying a booth by herself, tearing sugar packets one at a time with elaborate precision and stirring in the contents. She was either grinning or grinding her teeth.

"Mind if I join?" Jez said, dropping onto the opposite seat, upholstered in that same tired red as the stools.

Vonda didn't look up. "Nope." Tonight she wore a winter camou T-shirt, irregular stripes of white and light blue and darker blue. It hugged her shoulders, her breasts.

The diner wasn't crowded enough for them to have to share the booth.

The waitress came halfway toward them, caught Jez's eye and raised a fine eyebrow. *Same as last time?* Jez's chin dipped in a shallow nod.

"How do you do that?" Vonda was blowing steam off the lip of her cup, having finished sugaring her coffee. She looked straight across at Jez.

The question meant Vonda knew what she was. Jez said, "I'm a regular here."

"Me too. But I have to order every time."

Jez shrugged. "Try tipping better."

A vein stood out on the back of Vonda's left hand. Her nails were dark crescents.

"Looked like you had some trouble getting into the lot." The big front window was behind Vonda.

"Assholes need to learn how to drive."

"Is it like that for you out on the road?"

Vonda took a slow sip of coffee. "On the road, I'm an angel in a power dive. You haul too?"

"I do."

Their meals arrived, and after that it was flirting and coy and ribald comments. The other customers in the diner had paid no attention when Vonda was here alone. Now Jez was aware of an increasing interest, tinged with discomfort. Was this another taboo, something she hadn't known beforehand? She was, after all, still relatively recently returned from the dead. People whose deaths were not overly traumatic had been spontaneously coming back for close to a year. That was time enough for subcultural rules to form.

Vonda sat back in the booth and pushed off her empty plate in the same movement. Her eyes flickered this way and that, taking in those other customers. Was she too aware of the attention? Probably not. It was very subtle.

"You hear statistics. So many die of heart attacks, such and such many keel over from blot clots. But they get tucked away in a morgue." Vonda shook her head with a deep dismay. "It's amazing to think how the sands of the human race just run naturally through the hourglass."

Jez said nothing. She didn't know how many here in the diner had expired naturally. Maybe it hadn't occurred to this woman that were alternate ways to meet one's death.

Vonda followed her back to her place, which was nearer. Then it was lips and grinding hips and busy fingers and tongues. When Jez had been out of work, she had taken up running to fill the time and had gotten herself back into pre-thirties shape. Vonda was a quivering bowstring, muscular, aggressive. The tension of the road was in her, and she was taking it all out on Jez, which was just fine.

After—and there were several *afters*, but this was the one where they finally spoke—Vonda asked, "How did you know I was a lesbian?"

Jez laughed, a brief but real guffaw, and she realized she hadn't laughed like that in . . . a while. Not *since*.

"What's funny?"

"I'm trying to remember when I last heard someone use that term."

In the crook of Jez's arm, Vonda was trying to decide whether to be angry or not.

"When I was in school," Jez explained, "mono-sexuals were given a hard time."

"Oh." The tension went out of Vonda's neck as she lay her head back down.

Jez wanted to ask her a question too. And she guessed that Vonda had more, far deeper questions for her as well; but maybe those would wait.

"How'd you get your job?" She named Vonda's sketchy little haulage company. "I applied there and got turned down flat, back when—" *Back when I was alive.* Unsaid words. But Vonda hadn't died, and they didn't share that unspoken understanding. All they had was the tacit empathy of newfound lovers.

Jez strongly suspected that Vonda wanted to ask her about her death. Jez wasn't ready to talk about that. She simply hoped Vonda would answer her more innocuous question.

She did. "I went to the office for twenty-eight days straight. My driving record should've got me hired, but it didn't. So I just wore 'em the fuck down."

Jez wondered if the same tactic would have worked for her. Probably not. Vonda Hupy had a special quality.

"You got a nice place. Real nice." Vonda was walking around the apartment now, bare feet on wood, *patpat-pat.* Jez leaned in a doorway and admired the flex of her taut ass. "My place is a sty. I never would've guessed you hauled if I'd seen all this." She gestured at brass fittings, at well-coordinated art on the walls.

Jez went to speak but found herself without enough breath for words. Vonda was staring at her, as if waiting.

Finally Jez said, "I want to see you again. I want more than this."

Vonda maintained that gaze awhile. Then, "I want that too."

They synchronized their trucks' grid systems, so that each knew where the other was on the road, without the guesswork or triangulation. Jez visited Vonda's apartment, and it was a sty pretty much. But it wasn't the cruddiness of neglect; rather, the result of a mind and body occupied with other priorities.

Vonda liked to draw. Vonda liked charcoal. Black specks swarmed in the air whenever something in her apartment was disturbed. The stuff was permanently under her fingernails. Deadtree sheets were scattered everyplace, and they bore the markings of her art. All of it was crude. All of it was forceful. Vonda worked with harsh lines. Her themes were vibrant, vital. She had something to say and said it insistently.

Jez loved her work.

"You don't get worked up about much, do you?" A smile played on Vonda's growly mouth. Her tone was a little bitter.

Jez had been enthusing for forty straight minutes over Vonda's art as the two of them sat cross-legged on dingy teal carpeting. "I feel like I haven't shut up about how much I like your work."

"You say less than you probably think you do." Vonda tilted toward her, kissed her smartly on the cheek. "It's okay."

There were still the other, far larger questions lingering and hovering. Jez could sense them in the charcoal-dusted air. She and this woman had been involved for several weeks now. Perhaps Jez could make the inevitable questioning easier on herself—and on Vonda as well.

"How," Jez asked softly, "did you know I was . . . dead?" It wasn't the preferred term. Actually, there was no term for what she was, nothing the world had yet agreed on. "At the diner that night."

Vonda held her face still a moment, then burst out with a laugh. "Guess the same way you knew I was gay."

Jez joined in the laughing, and it felt good. Then she stopped, and waited.

After a time Vonda grew quiet, and after a long thoughtful pause she said, "Can you tell me how it was? When . . . when you were— When you *weren't*? Shit! I don't know how to ask this."

Jez nodded, then thought to say, "It's okay." She'd had a while to prepare for this. She was nervous. Less nervous than she would have been before her death. But more nervous here with Vonda than she would have been with anyone else. It was because she cared deeply for the woman.

She'd been sitting on this rug too long. Half her butt was asleep. She shifted.

"It's being frozen inside a fish bowl, sapphire ice all about. It is a pulse, a newborn's, very very fast. It's salt, hot salt, like seawater on an old piling under a blazing summer sun. It's a memory of melting snow. The hurtling of a comet on a billion year suicide plunge. It's vertigo. It's claustrophobia. It is . . ."

She stopped.

Vonda lifted her shoulders, an elaborate shrug. "I guess it really can't be described, then. You've been to the other side. You've seen what happens after a person kicks off. And it's nothing but freshman poetry."

They kissed, and this time it was Jez releasing excess energy, aggressively, and Vonda accommodated her as they made love on that dismal carpet.

Jez, though, knew Vonda had one last momentous question yet to voice. But perhaps she wouldn't ask it.

It was a lot of dock to depot runs. Several harbors lay within the tri-state region, and many warehouses awaited that cargo. The night, if anything, improved Jez. Certainly she had by now adjusted to nighttime driving. She was also used to the people she interacted with. She felt at ease among her kind.

However, now and again she grew aware of a mild extra scrutiny, what would have been a stink-eye look from strangers in her old life. Some knew her before she knew them: a reputation, preceding. She had a live girlfriend. *Live.*

But no one said anything to her, no censures, no condemnations. She was of a category of human being who no longer needed constant explicit words.

A month after she had failed—as every other returnee had similarly failed—to explain the afterlife to her lover,

Vonda asked the other question. The one of equal or greater enormity. Certainly the question Jez thought of as the most dangerous.

They were at Jez's place. One of Vonda's charcoals, framed and behind glass, hung on the front room's wall. The brunette woman had brought other objects into the apartment, little lifeline things which reminded Jez of her presence when she wasn't here.

Vonda asked her question when Jez wasn't expecting it, at a casual moment without solemn prelude. Vonda was lacing up her boots, getting ready to go out to work.

"Can I ask you something?"

"Sure," Jez said, sitting up in bed, sipping a second glass of wine. Drinking alone. Vonda had to drive; she didn't.

"How'd you die?" No dramatic lead-in pause, no dire tone.

Jez looked at her. Vonda slowly combed a handful of dark disarrayed hair off her forehead with her fingers.

Half a dozen lies sprang to mind, convincing falsehoods. Jez had rehearsed some of these. There were many ways a person could lose her life and then come back. If the death event wasn't too physiologically damaging, existence would be automatically restored. So this very strange, paradigm-upending past year had demonstrated to the world.

But instead of one of the lies, Jezebel Canha told her lover the truth. She had intentionally taken her own life.

It wasn't a long explanation. She laid out her reasons and how she had accomplished her passing. Vonda said nothing, and continued to stare. Jez started to add to her accounting but stopped herself. Despite the wine, her gut had gone cold.

She heard Vonda grinding her teeth a few seconds before she said, "You *killed* yourself for a fuckin' job!"

"I had to—"

"You *didn't* fucking have to! I got work without resorting to throwing my life away. That's disgusting, Jez! I can't believe you would do that."

Vonda's jacket lay over a chair in the bedroom. She spun, marched toward it and swung her arm, a boxer's pile-driving punch, but with an open hand so to claw up her leather jacket before she stalked out of the room, stomped down the apartment's entryway, and slammed the front door.

It was a primal reaction, something from deep inside the species. Jez knew this. She understood Vonda Hupy's response. It was why she had been reluctant to share this information. She remembered the dismayed look in Vonda's eyes as she'd looked around the diner that night, wondering at all the dead people.

Jez couldn't explain what death was like. Neither could she tell the woman she loved how sensible it had been for her to overdose on potassium chloride. She didn't regret what she had done.

But it terrified her to think she might have lost Vonda. True terror, the emotion brighter and more vivid than anything she had felt since her return to the living.

She'd had two generous glasses of chardonnay. Her truck wouldn't let her drive like this. She phoned Vonda, but even her voicemail was off. She snatched up her personal datascroll and accessed the grid. Vonda was heading for the nearest harbor. Jez, looking at the screen and biting her lip, saw how fast she was traveling. She must be burning up the night road. She was an excellent driver, with expert control of her rig.

But Jez remembered her in the diner parking lot, aggressive, keyed up, using her truck to express her volatility.

She was still staring at the datascroll. Several seconds went by.

Vonda's rig was still on the highway, but it was no longer moving.

She had to take a taxi out there.

Black and yellow wreckage was strewn across two lanes. Another vehicle had been involved in the accident, but the driver was unhurt. One southbound lane of the roadway remained open.

Paramedics were already there, but other emergency services continued to arrive. Jez's taxi waited, in the breakdown lane.

She had no legal right to inquire about Vonda Hupy's condition; so a Highway Patrolwoman told her in calm tones. But that officer made no effort to stop her approaching the ambulance, and the medical technicians, equally composed, let her near enough to the gurney to see that this wasn't a death from which anyone could come back.

The broken scattering of metal and metaplastic reminded Jez of the floors in Vonda's apartment, disordered with her charcoal'ed sheets of paper.

The night was chilly enough to make cool tracks of the tears on her cheeks. Unaware of them until now, she staggered back from the scene of destruction. None of the civilian traffic passing in the lone clear lane slowed down to gawk. The emergency personnel on hand didn't look upon her in judgment. Her cabdriver didn't step out to hurry her along.

They understood. And even if some suspected her relationship with the formerly live woman from the truck, no one reproached her for it. All of them on the scene, every last one, had experienced—however briefly—the unexplainable reality which awaited humans after death, and that experience had given them all a unique forbearance.

Jez wiped her eyes and walked toward the breakdown lane, where the taxi still waited.

CONTRIBUTORS

Nathan Batchelor

Nathan lives in and writes fiction from Columbus, Ohio. He has sold more than a dozen stories to magazines across the world. He is currently in a creative writing MFA program at Ashland University.

You can find him on twitter @NateBatchelor.

Eric Del Carlo

Eric Del Carlo's short fiction has appeared in *Asimov's*, *Analog*, *Clarkesworld* and many other publications. He co-wrote the urban fantasy novel *The Golden Gate Is Empty* with his father, Victor Del Carlo.

Find him on Facebook for questions and comments.

Tori Fredrick

Tori Fredrick is a librarian specializing in reader services, a northern transplant to North Carolina, and a lifetime horror fan (with an incredibly strong stomach). By enthusiast standards she has a moderately sized Tarot collection and is very honored that her second fiction publication is appearing in *Underland Arcana*.

H. L. Fullerton

H. L. Fullerton writes fiction—mostly speculative, occasionally about being haunted—which can be found in more than 50 anthologies and magazines including *Mysterion*, *Translunar Travelers Lounge*, and *Lackington's*, and is the author of the somewhat haunting novella: *The Boy Who Was Mistaken for a Fairy King*.

You may follow them on Twitter at @ByHLFullerton

Selah Janel

Selah Janel has written many e-books, including *Mooner*, *The Ruins of St. Louis*, *The Inheritance*, and *Candles*. Her work has appeared in anthologies including *The Grotesquerie* and *The Big Bad volumes 1 & 2*, as well as publications such as *Electric Spec* and *Siren's Call*. An unrepentant theater geek, she worked for over twenty years in theater and entertainment building and designing costumes in regional theater, holiday events, amusement parks, and haunted events.

Keep up with her and her work at www.selahjanel.com, www.facebook.com/authorSJ, or @SelahJanel on Twitter.

Jon McGoran

Jon McGoran is the award-winning author of ten novels for adults and young adults including the YA science fiction thrillers *Spliced*, *Splintered*, and *Spiked* (Holiday House Books), as well as the acclaimed ecological thrillers *Drift*, *Deadout*, and *Dust Up* (Tor/Forge). Both *Spliced* and *Splintered* have been honored by American Bookseller's Association as ABC Best Books for Young Readers. His other books include the D. H. Dublin forensic thrillers *Body Trace*, *Blood Poison*, and *Freezer Burn* (Berkley/

Penguin) and *The Dead Ring* (Titan Books), based on the TV show, *The Blacklist*.

He has published numerous short stories, including "Bad Debt," which won an honorable mention in *Best American Mystery Stories 2014*. He is a freelance writer, developmental editor, writing coach, and cohost of The *Liars Club Oddcast*, a podcast about writing and creativity.

For more, visit www.jonmcgoran.com.

Linda McMullen

Linda McMullen is a wife, mother, diplomat, and homesick Wisconsinite. Her short stories and the occasional poem have appeared in over ninety literary magazines. She received Pushcart and Best of the Net nominations in 2020.

She may be found on Twitter: @LindaCMcMullen.

W. T. Paterson

W. T. Paterson is a three-time Pushcart Prize nominee, holds an MFA in Fiction Writing from the University of New Hampshire, and is a graduate of Second City Chicago. His work has appeared in over 90 publications worldwide including *The Saturday Evening Post, The Forge Literary Magazine, The Delhousie Review, Brilliant Flash Fiction*, and *Fresh Ink*. A semi-finalist in the Aura Estra short story contest, his work has also received notable accolades from Lycan Valley, North 2 South Press, and Lumberloft. He spends most nights yelling for his cat to "Get down from there!"

Visit his website at www.wtpaterson.com.

Lexi Pérez

Lexi Perez is a junkie of all genres, but will always find a home in the dark and twisty. She is inspired by authors like Neil Gaiman and Stephen King, and loves finding cool rocks on hikes. Her hobbies include crochet, knitting, embroidery, and needle felting. Lexi lives in Denver with her partner and cat.

Jennifer Quail

Jennifer Quail is a writer of fantasy, horror, and mystery, a wine-tasting consultant, trivia geek, and owner of two of the world's cutest dogs. In December 2019 she achieved a lifelong dream of appearing on *Jeopardy!* without embarrassing herself in the process. She enjoys travel, art, and excessive amounts of coffee.

Find more at authorjenniferquail.com.

PAMELA COLMAN SMITH

The tarot images in this issue of Arcana are from the deck illustrated by Pamela Colman Smith. It was released in 1909 as the Rider-Waite deck (so named, at that time, in reference to its publisher, William Rider & Son). It remains the most influential and widely used tarot deck. While the impetus for the deck came from Arthur Edward Waite, Colman Smith was responsible for the iconography of the cards.

Pamela Colman Smith also illustrated over twenty books, wrote two collections of Jamaican folklore, edited two magazines, and ran the Green Sheaf Press, a small press devoted to women writers. She continued to write and illustrate throughout her life.

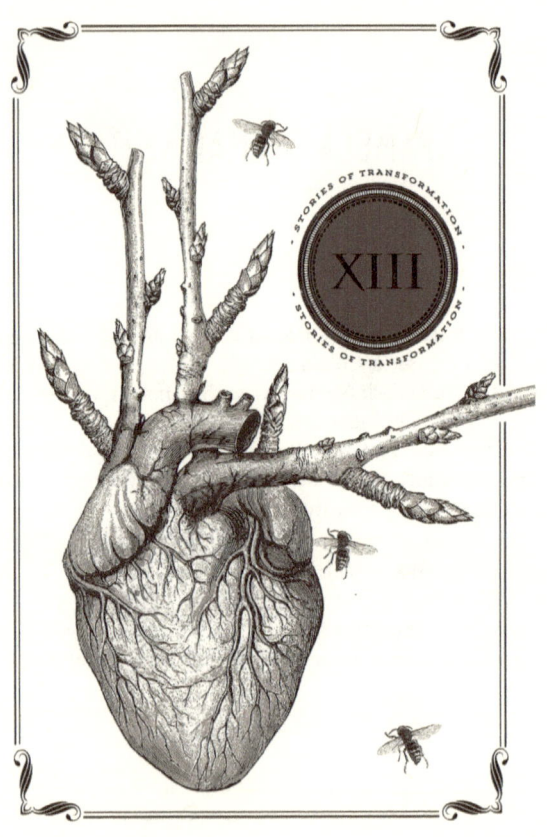

STORIES OF TRANSFORMATION

XIII

STORIES OF TRANSFORMATION

XIII

The thirteenth Tarot card is Death, and he is a symbol not of the end, but of transformation and rebirth. This is the genesis and root of *Thirteen: Stories of Transformation*. The twenty-eight authors of this collection are voices—new and old—who are not afraid to explore what comes next. Whether it be a life after death, a life without love, a life filled with hunger, or the life shared by a ghost. These are stories of the weird, the mythic, the fantastic, the futuristic, the supernatural, and the horrific.

With stories by Liz Argall • M. David Blake • Richard Bowes • George Cotronis • Amanda C. Davis • Julie C. Day • Jetse de Vries • Jennifer Giesbrecht • Daryl Gregory • Rik Hoskin • Rebecca Kuder • Claude Lalumière • Marc Levinthal • Grá Linnaea • Alex Dally MacFarlane • Juli Mallett • Lyn McConchie • Fiona Moore • Gregory L. Norris • Adrienne J. Odasso • Cat Rambo • Andrew Penn Romine • David Tallerman • Tais Teng Richard Thomas • Fran Wilde • A. C. Wise • Christie Yant

Edited by Mark Teppo.

Available at independent bookstores everywhere.

http://www.underlandpress.com

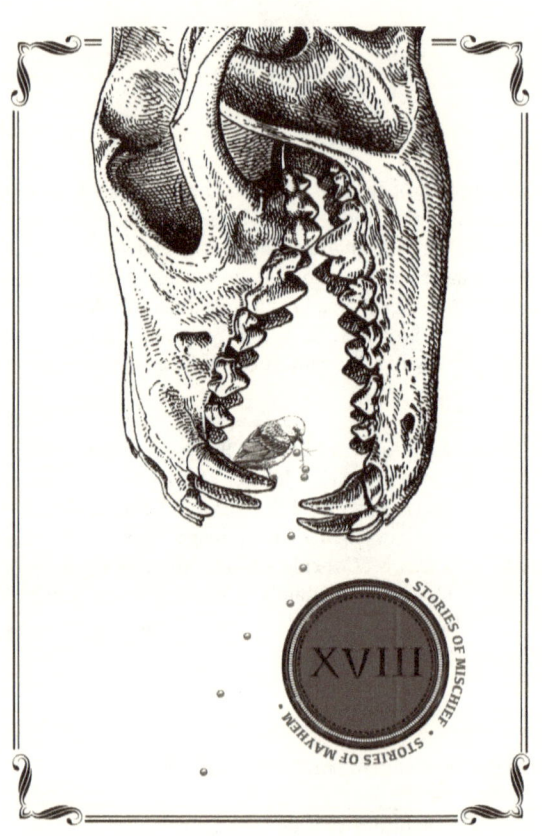

XVIII

STORIES OF MISCHIEF · STORIES OF MAYHEM ·

XVIII

The eighteenth Tarot card is the Moon, and those who raise their arms to her know she offers Mercy and Severity in equal measure. This is the great river at night, where wolves howl and all doors are open. All futures are possible, and every truth is elusive. This is the source and passion of *Eighteen: Stories of Mischief & Mayhem*. These twenty-four stories from voices—old and new—celebrate the inevitability of fate, the horror of prophecy, and the shivering delight of not knowing what comes next.

Cross over the threshold with us, and explore the strange, the weird, and the fantastic. Do not fear what lies ahead. It is the same as what came before. The only difference is you. This is *Eighteen*, and nothing will be the same.

With stories by Forrest Aguirre • Darin Bradley • Christopher East • Scott Edelman • Nicole Feldringer • Ben Gamblin • Ingrid Garcia • A. P. Howell • Emma Johnson-Rivard • E. E. King • Jessie Kwak • Shannon Lawrence • Gerri Leen • Mark Mills • Christi Nogle Tammie Painter • Josh Rountree • Erica Sage • Lorraine Schein • J. Dee Stanley • Richard Thomas • John Waterfall • Wendy N. Wagner • Todd Zack

Edited by Mark Teppo.

Available at independent bookstores everywhere.

http://www.underlandpress.com

www.ingramcontent.com/pod-product-compliance
Lightning Source LLC
Chambersburg PA
CBHW050404110726
47899CB00008B/2643